Oldrich paced the room and stared out the window onto Central Park. Finally he went to the refrigerator for a second bottle of beer. From the closet he took a suitcase and opened it on his bed.

The suitcase was full of boxes containing, as its custom slip said, costume jewelry: necklaces, tiaras, and bracelets of gaudy paste set in gold-plated bronze. He removed one large box.

He drank some more. Then he lifted the top off the box and set it beside the bottle. Only when the last of the bottle was poured into his glass did Oldrich allow himself to look directly at the red-gold bows, green-gold diadem, gems and enamel, and distinctly crooked cross that marked the crown of Saint Stephen's, the Holy Crown of Hungary . . .

CANTO FOR A GYPSY

Also by Martin Cruz Smith
Published by Ballantine Books

GORKY PARK

GYPSY IN AMBER

CANTO FOR A GYPSY

Martin Cruz Smith

BALLANTINE BOOKS • NEW YORK

Saint Stephen's Crown, also known as the
Holy Crown of Hungary, is real. All the
characters in this book are fictitious.

Library of Congress Catalog Card Number: 72-79529

ISBN 0-345-30615-5

This edition published by arrangement with G. P. Putnam's Sons

Manufactured in the United States of America

First Ballantine Books Edition: January 1983

For Bob and Dolly

If in the morning a Gypsy you meet,
The rest of your day will be lucky and sweet,
But if the black-robed priest comes first,
Your luck is gone, expect the worst.

—AN OLD SAYING OF THE ROM

LASSU

CHAPTER
1

ST. PATRICK'S LAY below them, sanctuary bounded by ambulatory and communion rail, pews like an endless repetition, faith overwhelmed by stone.

The priest had viewed the sacristy and all twenty chapels and he was happy to relax in the cool of the high gallery above the business of worship. His tour guide, an usher with enamel American flag in his lapel, uttered judgment.

"The women are the worst."

The priest raised his eyebrows in mock outrage.

"Sure," the usher went on. "They come in, sit down behind some other woman who's praying and switch purses. We have to put chains through the candlesticks or they'd walk off with those."

"A regular hotbed of crime, you'd say. But you were telling me about the funeral services for Senator Kennedy."

"That's right. There were Secret Service men where we are and on the other galleries and in the organ loft. They took over our room for their headquarters," he said with reminiscent irritation. "They knew this place inside out."

The priest mused, watching a fish school of Japanese tourists following their guide with cameras and notebooks.

"Wouldn't an assassin be able to do that, too?" he wondered. "Get the building plans?"

"Nooo. To get a copy from the City Building Department you got to have a written letter of permission from the cathedral administrator."

"Ah." The priest straightened up. He was middle-aged but fit and his mustache raised suspicions in the usher that he might have a hippy parish. The priest had earlier remarked that the maintenance men all seemed to be black or Spanish. "Well, thank you for the tour, Mr. Grimm. By the way, did they have handguns or rifles?"

The usher was taken aback.

"Up here? Rifles. It was like a military operation."

"Of course, it was."

The priest used a side door to reach the adjacent administration building. The administrator was not in and the ladies at the reception desk told the priest he would need an appointment to see the monsignor when he returned.

"I just saw him," the priest said. "He told me to wait in his office."

"Really, father, the monsignor is impossible. What's the point of having a secretary?"

"May I?"

He walked into the administrator's office.

The office window was above the eye level of pedestrians on Madison Avenue. In the outer office a typewriter carriage snapped sideways with exasperated force.

He pulled the desk drawer open and removed stationery, envelopes and a personal note with a good sample of the monsignor's signature.

CHAPTER
2

THE FIRST GREAT diaspora of Indian outcasts called Rom began about 1000 A.D. They traveled in wagons, mended metalware, spoke a form of Sanskrit and told fortunes. Some went through Palestine and around the African coast to cross with the Moors into Spain. They became known as Gitanos. The northern migration went through Byzantium to the Balkans. In the region of Moldo-Walachia, now Hungary and Rumania, they were hunted and enslaved, but enough escaped by the fourteenth century to infest Western Europe. Usually they carried fraudulent letters from His Holiness the Pope asking Christian princes to welcome the exotic aliens. They were pilgrims from the Holy Land sentenced to wander, so the letters went, for a lapse of faith. Since the letters claimed their origin to be Egypt, they were known as Egyptians, then 'Gyptians and finally Gypsies.

In Spain were the Gitanos. In the rest of the continent, Kalderash Gypsies raised the function of goldsmith and armorer to near occult status. The Sinti, named for their origin on the banks of the Sind, spread from the Low Countries to the Black Sea, and a tribe of wild cutthroats called Tshurari moved north to terrorize the Russian highways.

The Lovari were the last tribe to escape from Hungary, which is why older Gypsy bands in France and Spain continue to call them Hongrois or Hungaros, but it was the Lovari who made the greatest impact. Not only were they smiths, musicians and fortune tellers, during peace they controlled Europe's horse markets and during war they formed mercenary armies. Queen Elizabeth ordered their death to a man, but she had better luck ridding her island of the Pope than of its Rom.

The first Gypsies to cross the Atlantic were Gitanos, camp followers with Cortez and Pizarro. The prouder Lovari arrived as condemned criminals, the French Rom shipped to Biloxi in the Louisiana territories and the English Rom to New England. Sentencing them to the New World was like giving birds the sky, and in time more tribes came voluntarily, some traveling so often between Old World and New that their names became hyphenated, like the Turko-Americans. By 1950, there were an estimated 50,000 Rom in the United States, but as a police captain detailed to them said at the time, he could no more guess how many pigeons were in a single tree.

As elsewhere, the American Rom added *gaja,* or non-Gypsy, names: Petulengro, or forgeworker, became Smith and Gry, or horse—for the man who dealt in them—became Grey.

As the rain passed and the heat returned, a Gypsy named Romano Gry was dispassionately doing away with an antique dealer called Roman Grey. He selected a serrated knife and cut into the heart of a styrofoam block, sawing it neatly in two.

Sweat dampened the cigarette in his lips and blue smoke softened the sharp features of his face. Exchanging the long knife for a short, two-edged stiletto, he hollowed out each half of the block. When he was done he had molds that fit loosely around a pair of ormolu candlesticks, leaving enough room for the chamois sacks that protected their gold-and-mercury skin, the Or Moulu. It was tedious work, but he didn't know how long his trip would take and the storage crates would have to be moved again if the police tried to impound them. He was taping the blocks back together when the front door opened and he heard his *gaja* name called.

Roman tapped the knife on his palm impatiently. The customer couldn't see him from the front room, and he would just wait until the man went away.

Up front, the customer surveyed a shop that looked like a museum turned flea market. Regence armchairs hung from the walls beside heliotrope rolls of Persian carpets. Meissen and Mennecy china appeared haphazardly in cases between silk prints and tapestries, any of which would have been displayed separately with dramatic lighting in another East Side shop. The only sign of life was a cat that ascended from an ottoman to a commode to the top of a partially restored Chippendale highboy. The customer took the cat's place on the ottoman with satisfaction. His pleasure was complete when he saw he was no longer alone.

The man who came from the back room was tall for a Gypsy and seemed larger because he was built along broad lines. Perspiration curled his black hair and gave a nimbus to the brown skin of a face that was more interesting than handsome. Roman had struck more than one visitor less as an antique dealer than a browsing barbarian. If this was the customer's reverie, one glance from the dealer's thoroughly realistic eyes told him to end it.

"You must be Mr. Grey."

"For another week. What can I do for you?"

"My name is John Killigan." He looked at the knife in Roman's hand. "I hope I'm not interrupting anything."

"Excuse me."

Roman laid the stiletto down and returned to scrutinize his visitor. John Killigan appeared to be in his middle sixties, a narrow, elegant man with white hair combed tightly back. The suit was expensive and, except for his shirt, he wore black from his shoes to the hat held in his long fingers.

"Do you mind if I sit?" Killigan asked after he'd settled back on the ottoman.

"I should tell you now, if there's anything special you want to order, I won't be able to help. I'm closing down the shop in a day or two."

Killigan was not dismayed.

"How long will you be gone?"

"I don't know."

"Just traveling or a business excursion?"

Roman almost smiled in spite of himself. The old man had nerve.

"That must be wonderful," Killigan went on without waiting for an answer. "Just picking up and traveling, not even knowing when you'll come back. I'm sixty-six, you know, and I've never just gone off by myself for fun. I suppose it's the effect of working for an institution. Your life's not your own that way."

"No, I guess not."

Roman was mildly curious because Killigan didn't seem a man whose trade was small talk. The Gypsy pulled up a chair and sat down. When he pulled a pack of Gauloise from his pocket, Killigan accepted one—another surprise.

"It strikes you as strange not leading one's own life," Killigan suggested. "You have to remember that you are the exception."

"You know," Roman replied, "the last person to say that to me was a very understanding detective. I'm afraid I didn't catch the name of your institution."

"There's far more I do not understand about you, Mr. Grey, but we'll get to know each other. You are an expert on all sorts of antiques, I understand. Articles of goldsmith work, for instance."

When Roman waited for further explanation, Killigan changed the subject.

"Have you ever been in Hungary?" he asked.

"Yes."

"Can you speak Hungarian?"

Roman nodded.

Killigan asked in Hungarian, "Have you ever been baptized a Catholic?"

"That and a few others," Roman answered in the same language, then switched to English. "What has this got to do with gold work? I'm not offended, but is it possible you're the executor of a will that stipulates only Hungarian-speaking Catholics can appraise the estate?"

"No, no," Killigan laughed. "Some pieces are coming

into my possession, though. I'd need an estimate and some-one to look after them for a week or two."

"It sounds like an auction house display. Parke-Bernet can handle that better than I can." He gestured around the shop. "If I tried to display something here, I'd never find it again."

"I have the display facilities."

"Your institution's facilities?"

"Yes."

Roman leaned forward.

"But you don't want to tell me the name of this mys-terious institution. Maybe you could say who recommended me, or just what pieces these are, or who made them?" He let time for an answer go by. "Mr. Killigan, this is not the most persuasive offer I've ever had."

"The remuneration would not be very high, either."

"You see what I mean? At any rate, I'm not going to be here, and there are at least fifty jewelers in the city who specialize in the auction trade."

"These jewels are different."

"Mr. Killigan, do you mind if I ask how much you know about jewelry?"

"Not very much. That's why I'm here."

"The great mass of jewelry in private hands is junk. The interesting pieces, Byzantine or Indian or Celtic, are almost all in museums. Even if I weren't going anywhere I wouldn't be interested in handling auction fodder."

"This is hardly fodder."

"I'm amazed." Roman shook his head. "You're still ask-ing me to do it. I didn't think even private bankers had that much confidence."

Killigan's amused blue eyes contrasted with his funereal suit.

"I can see you have your principles, Mr. Grey." As he stood to go, the cat stirred and caught his eye. "By the way, I see you're restoring this highboy. Just hypothetically, how would one go about making a fake of an antique like this?"

Roman stepped out to the piece in question. Absent-mindedly, he stroked the cat.

"There is no way."

"But people do, I've read. Don't they choose some old worm-eaten wood and work with that?"

"They try," Roman told him. "But as soon as they take the old finish off, they find the wood gets more worm-eaten and rotted. You can't put a new face on something that's rotting on the inside no matter how clever you are."

Killigan paused in thought.

"You won't take this estate for me?"

"I'll be gone."

"That's in the hands of God."

"Then that would be a change," Roman remarked as they shook hands.

Before he left, Killigan reached up to give the cat a long stroke down its black back.

"A beautiful animal. What's his name?"

"Beng."

"Beng?" Killigan put his hat on as Roman opened the door. "The devil's name, isn't it?"

"How did you know?"

"I don't get around much for pleasure but I have traveled, in the line of business. Good-bye."

He left, and Roman watched him walk down the street, a tall, thin figure in black moving past the row of town houses in long, jaunty strides.

Alone again, Roman worked until five crates of candlesticks, services and clocks lined the back room. He was tying up the first of the rugs when Kore arrived.

Lovari like Roman, Kore was a giant with curly red hair that sprouted from under a stained fedora. All Kore's clothes suffered a similar fate: the height of fashion when bought, wrinkled the day after and worn until they fell apart. It was an expensive habit but it made sense on long trips, and with the seashell amulet he wore around his neck it lent Kore a primitive panache. For the past week he'd moved Roman's crates to a warehouse in Queens, so he poured himself a glass of steaming tea and sat in a groaning sidechair without asking.

"*Aukko tu pios adrey Romanes,*" he toasted Roman, lifting the strong tea to his lips.

Roman, a rope between his teeth, straddled a rolled-up rug. It was a Broussa, heavy silk interwoven with copper threads and a little more pliable than a floor board. Kore removed a glossy fold-out advertisement from his jacket and read: " 'For the man of distinction the final step up.' Huh! I had my first Cadillac when I was fifteen."

He opened the flyer to its fullest width and looked at an artist's conception of an Eldorado set among the gentry of a yacht marina.

"I think I want one with a bar. How do you think those Spanish Gypsies will like it when we drive into Barcelona in a car with a bar? Those Gitanos will slit their throats. We can choose any girls we want. You take a singer and I'll take a dancer and they can pay our way for the rest of the trip. What do you think of my idea, Romano?"

Roman manhandled the rug into a tighter roll. Globules of perspiration joined each other on his face and neck.

"Persian." Kore looked at the rug authoritatively.

"Turkish," Roman grunted through the rope.

Kore sniffed. He scooped some strawberry jam into his tea and mixed it with his finger, ignoring the heat.

"You don't like my idea about the Spanish girls? You insist on taking that *gaja* girl with you?"

Roman grunted again. The rug was tight as a cylinder. He reached around it for the rope in his mouth.

"Going to teach her how to tell fortunes? How to pick pockets, eh? Make her into a real *Romani* chi? I bet!" Kore's eyes narrowed. "Ah, what a Rom you used to be. That was before you became a rug merchant, of course. Now look at you, so weak you can't even roll a carpet."

Roman's hand missed and the rope fell to the floor. Kore got out of the chair and walked around Roman, observing his one-handed efforts to retrieve the rope with disinterest.

"I can see you five years from now. No more traveling with the Rom. You'll be selling televisions then, a weak little *gajo* with no color to his skin. My God, you are having trouble with that rug, aren't you, little brother?"

"Would you like to help?" Roman asked evenly.

"Just give it to me."

Kore took his time finding a place to set his glass down before putting out his massive hands to take the carpet. Roman waited until Kore had a good grip, then let go. The heavy rug flew open with the strength of a copper coil, knocking Kore's hat off. A yard of brilliant carpet undulated in the air as Kore staggered around the room like Laocoön, trying to keep more from unraveling. Roman leaned on a crate and sipped from Kore's half-finished glass of tea.

"Go on, you ignorant thief of parked cars, what were you saying?"

"Help me, for God's sake!"

"Quite a weave, isn't it? Those six hundred knots to the square inch and the copper give it a certain integrity. But why am I telling an expert like you?"

"Avata acai!"

"I don't think you need any help. You're strangling it very nicely." He put the empty glass down. "Good luck. This rug merchant has other things to do."

"Romano, where are you going?" Kore called. "Romano, *as Develesky!*"

Roman wandered into the front room, checking what else Kore could take with him to the warehouse. But his mind was half out of the shop and the city, on a road where the country passed slowly, the air was suffused with rose paprika and the only camps were those of friends.

The trouble was that Kore was right. This time Dany made it different.

CHAPTER
3

IN RETURN FOR a request on stolen church stationery with a simple tracing of Administrator Burns' signature, Odrich received copies of St. Patrick's foundation, plumbing and electrical plans from the city archives. He studied them for three days and returned to the cathedral on the last night.

The cardinal's residence was a mirror image of the administration building. A patrolman kept an informal duty on the sidewalk, and Odrich was sure that the doors and windows would be connected to the local precinct house.

Odrich turned the corner of Madison to Fiftieth Street. At Fiftieth and Fifth there was another patrolman. Odrich went up the steps to the entrance of St. Patrick's south transept. In the shadow of the church door, he studied the rear face of the cardinal's house.

The residence was three stories high. A private covered passageway from it almost touched the church. The rest of the face was a sampler of Victorian carving, particularly the window bays and gables. Twin Moorish windows on the second floor were topped by a single Gothic window, and

flanking both was a two-story window with a gable that
touched the roof line.

Odrich ran at the stone passage. His hands caught the
top and he rolled up over it. He lay on his stomach while
a patrolman walked from the corner to the middle of the
block, turned and went back. There were lights in the room
with the Moorish windows. He looked in and saw a man
at a writing desk. A fire engine wailed its way up Madison
without disturbing the writer's concentration. Odrich
grabbed the stone gutter above the window and hoisted
himself past it. He only had to walk up the side of the large
gable and he was on the roof.

The roof contained an air-conditioning unit, a chimney
and an exit from the top floor. The exit door had no outside knob, but he was delighted to find its lock was no more
than what he would have put on a bathroom. Using a
plastic credit card, he chivied it open.

The third floor was a work area and a library. On the
second he saw a light from the room he'd passed on the
way up. He padded down the stairs to the first-floor offices.

The cardinal's office was the largest and the least decorated. An immense desk sat between two windows, and
outside he could see the patrolman on his beat.

One drawer was locked, and Odrich went immediately
for that, using his credit card again rather than bothering
to pick it. As he jerked the card up, the drawer popped
out. He waited, holding it. Nobody came down the stairs.
Instead, he heard the flush of water pipes.

The list he was looking for was on top. One name was
checked.

He left the list in the drawer. It took him twenty minutes
to reach the roof again and go down the way he'd come.
On Fifth Avenue, he took a cab to his rooms at the Plaza.

After removing a congratulatory bottle of cold Würz-
burger from the suite's refrigerator, he called the Commodore Hotel. There were no indications that he had been
scaling a building, no crease in his summer suit or a lock
of his silver hair out of place. He wore a wristwatch but
no rings that might snag when he climbed. His face was
tanned and powerful, with gray eyes as deep-set and
patient as a doll's.

The phone was answered in Italian.

"The pictures are still drying in the bathroom."

"The films?" Odrich asked.

"Tomorrow. We had to take those to a laboratory. Is there anything else?"

"I have a name for you." Odrich wrote it in the condensation of the glass as he spoke. "Roman Grey. Find out where his shop is so we can pay him a call."

There was a hesitation on the other end.

"Won't that be difficult? To influence him, I mean?"

"Any antique dealer is a fraud; it's the nature of the business, Jozsef. I imagine we can offer him enough money. If we can't, that's his misfortune."

"I already found the black boy you wanted."

"Very good. Keep him around, in case."

"Is that all?"

"No," Odrich answered after a moment's thought. "The chief of security, Reggel. I've decided it would be wiser to put him out of the way if possible. It can look political or like an accident."

After hanging up, the tension persisted in Odrich. He paced the room and stared out the window onto Central Park. Finally, he went to the refrigerator for a second bottle of beer. From the closet he took a suitcase and opened it on his bed.

The suitcase was full of boxes containing, as its customs slips said, costume jewelry: necklaces, tiaras and bracelets of gaudy paste set in gold-plated bronze. He removed one large box.

He drank some more, not so much for the taste of the beer as to prolong the moment. Then he lifted the top off the box and set it beside the bottle. The newspaper padding inside he laid by the pillow. Only when the last of the bottle was poured into his glass did Odrich allow himself to look directly at the red-gold bows, green-gold diadem, gems and enamel, and distinctively crooked cross that marked the crown as Saint Stephen's, the Holy Crown of Hungary.

CHAPTER 4

DANY MURRAY WORE a bathrobe of Roman's as she dropped clothes piece by piece into a suitcase. She had wide-apart hazel eyes, brown hair as shiny as a page in *Vogue*, full lips pouted in thought and long legs that unconsciously stood, shifted and stood according to the basic poses of the professional model. Every move was as mindlessly graceful as a swan's and every move was a lie about the girl inside. Habit was hard, though. Roman was allowing her only one small suitcase for the car, and she had already packed it ten times. After each practice she looked at the closet, and the model in her was appalled to see the absolutely essential items she was leaving behind: Bill Blass boots, a hair dryer and Valentino slacks, just to mention a few.

"Why doesn't Kore like me?" she asked. "Does he think I'm going to slow you down?"

The answer was in Romany. Dany left the pyramid of clothes and went into the living room. Roman was at his desk making an inventory of the antiques left in the apartment.

"Could you say that again?"

"I thought you were trying to learn Romany."

"Sometimes I understand everything. That one I didn't."

"It's simple, Dany. The *tu* is the same as French."

"You know I can't speak French. Where is a girl going to learn French in Detroit?"

He sighed.

"You're angry," she said. It was warm and Roman was stripped to the waist. She massaged his shoulders.

"I'm not angry. I'm just wondering who the hell you're going to talk to besides me when we get there."

Dany was unfazed. She was happy talking to Roman.

"Tell me again where we're going," she asked.

"Barcelona. Sofia. Budapest."

A little unease crept into her stomach but she kept a game smile.

"You know, Gypsies would make marvelous spies."

She placed her hands on his head and watched her fingers snake through the black coils of his hair. It was blacker than black, she thought, blacker than color could be.

"You're happy I'm coming, aren't you?"

Roman laid his pencil aside and twisted around in his chair. He pulled an edge of the bathrobe aside and kissed her breast.

"I'm taking you because I love you. Is that enough? Now, will you go finish your packing? And don't worry about taking bras. Nobody who's anybody in Gypsy *kumpanias* is wearing them this year."

He squeezed her leg. Dany laughed and stepped away.

"Okay, I forget what I came in here to ask you, anyway."

Roman watched her walk out of the room and continued staring at the empty doorway.

A fashion model wouldn't last long on the road with a *kumpania* of Gypsies. In New York he was half *gaja*. That was the in-between man she wanted to marry. She had to know that life wasn't lived in an apartment furnished with the expensive overflow from his shop. That reality was a car driven all night from one border to another to avoid police, plumbing consisting of the nearest river and Gypsies a people who would regard her as an outsider and a fool. It was strange languages, dirt and monotonous danger. She wouldn't break during the first month, despite Kore's predictions, because she had determination. But determination would take her only so far. Her fascination of Rom would turn to disgust. Their car would carry the stench of sweat and anger. She wouldn't fight, she would just go home. Roman knew it as certainly as he knew at this moment she couldn't believe it would ever happen. That was why he was taking her, because she didn't believe him. And if he didn't go, he would lose more than Dany.

"I won't give myself away by talking," she called from the bedroom. "I'll just sit and smolder like the other Gypsy girls."

The doorbell rang. Roman closed the bedroom door before he answered it.

It was Kore with two teen-age boys. The boys entered excitedly, gawking at the spectacular collection of antiques.

"They want to come along," Kore reported.

"The Petulengro brothers, aren't they?"

The boys' dark eyes grew, amazed someone so famous in their small world knew who they were. They looked around the room again with respect that one man could steal so much.

"They saved some money from putting up bill posters," Kore said.

"I drive the car," the smaller boy explained. "John runs out and puts the poster up. We can do three hundred in a day and we've never been caught."

"Only their grandmother is alive, so they haven't been on the road for years. That's no way for boys to grow up, staying in one place," Kore pointed out. "How can they be expected to know other families unless they leave home?"

"Besides, the lawyer said we'd have to go to jail no matter how old we are if we get caught again."

"I thought you never got caught," Roman reminded him.

"But that was for stripping cars," the taller boy replied. "It's John—he can't run as fast as I can."

"They were caught taking the transmission from a car outside some embassy." Kore held his hand out. "They told the fellow from the embassy what he could do. Would you believe he understood Romany? But the judge wouldn't have recognized them if they were on the road."

Dany had been listening from the other side of the bedroom door without understanding a word of the conversation. She opened the door and came in, discreetly changed from the bathrobe to a pantsuit. When she saw the boys, she smiled.

"I heard some talking," she told Roman.

"This is John and Racki Petulengro. They'll be going with us."

Racki turned and asked Kore a question in Romany. Kore started to answer as coolly as he dared in front of Roman.

"Yes, I am going," Dany answered for him.

Kore and the boys almost gaped. In the next second they were in control again, but she had her moment of pride.

"Dany is my *chi*," Roman told them.

Odrich operated with an instrument shaped like a dental pick. Once the pick had wedged a tumbler aside he snapped his wrist, leaving a centimeter of soft metal that held the tumbler clear. It took Odrich no more than a minute to subvert the lock, and no early morning passersby disturbed him or the four men with him. The men followed Odrich into the antique shop, and he cleaned the lock from the inside. Beng ran out of the back room crying for breakfast.

"What should we do about the cat?"

"Don't kill it," Odrich said. "Find something for it to eat; it's hungry."

The front room had a haphazard flavor that annoyed Odrich. He went into the rear of the antique shop and found crates ready for packing. The cat's bowl, he noticed, was Spode.

"There is some very good stuff here," Jozsef said. He, like the others with Odrich, was in his middle thirties and had the clean-cut robustness of an Olympic athlete.

"Run like a junk shop. I can't understand why they chose a man like him." Odrich felt a growing distaste for the faceless Roman Grey. He set a chair next to the door to the front room. "We can wait here."

"What will you offer him?"

"Whatever he asks," Odrich answered. "It doesn't matter."

Beside his chair was a bucket of more Spode ware and water. He dipped a finger in the water and tasted it. Baking soda. Next to the bucket was a cluttered toolbox. He picked up a long serrated knife from it and put it back when he saw a short stiletto.

"If Grey does prove to be a saint, Jozsef, use this instead of your own. I'm sure he hasn't been informed yet. People will think it was nothing more than a robbery, or perhaps a connoisseur driven mad by this mess."

He leaned back so that he could see the window and door without being seen. The others played with the cat.

Five minutes had elapsed when Beng suddenly ran to the window.

"Here he is," Odrich whispered.

He watched a dark man cross the street to the shop.

"My God! He's a Gypsy," Odrich exclaimed. "What could be better?"

Beng pressed his face against the window and purred. Roman tapped the window and smiled. He unlocked the door and began turning the knob.

"Remember, let him get back here."

Roman looked to the side, his smile widening. A short man in a suit that seemed to be off the wrong rack crossed in front of the other window and the two men shook hands.

"Nothing helps business like a detective loitering around," Roman said loudly.

The detective's round face went from bland to embarrassed.

"I came to say good-bye and good luck."

Roman slapped the detective on the back.

"Come on in and have some tea. You can keep me company while I pack."

"Damn," Odrich whispered.

The one holding the knife put it away and, like the others, took out a .22 automatic.

"Some other time," the detective replied.

"Okay. But I have to start working if I'm ever going to get out of here."

Roman unlocked the door and pushed it open.

"Come on," Odrich urged.

A hand on his arm stopped Roman. The friendliness in his eyes cooled.

"Why didn't you say you came here on police business? Come in and look at the bills of sale if you want. You're not going to find any mistakes now, though."

They stopped breathing in the back room. Beng jumped to the door and tried to paw the door farther open.

"It's nothing like that," the detective tried to explain. "You have to take a ride with me."

"An arrest?"

"No. I got this call to pick you up. I really was coming to wish you luck anyway. Look, we're not going to headquarters, so don't worry about that."

"Sergeant Isadore, I'm not moving from this spot until you tell me where you want to take me."

"Roman," the detective flushed, "Roman, I'm taking you to church."

The antique dealer regarded his nonplussed friend. Finally, he shut the door and locked it. The two men went off together.

Odrich got out of his chair.

"That eliminates him. He would talk and the detective would listen. A peculiar pair." He turned his attention to the others. "Clean up the cat's bowl and put it where you found it. I want to see this boy you found. He'll have to do now."

On the way out, frustration inspired him to think about killing the cat.

"No," he corrected himself aloud, "best to leave this alone."

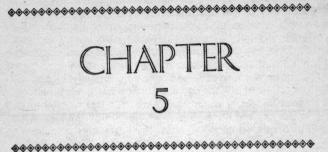

CHAPTER
5

JOHN CARDINAL KILLANE crossed the few steps between St. Patrick's and his residence, distance enough for him to change from confessor to ecclesiastical prince. He let himself in by his private passage and stepped into a hall decorated with children's drawings of the saints. One that seemed to have four legs and no head had him stumped. He would have asked his staff, but they were suspicious enough of him already. He couldn't afford not to know his headless saints.

A plate of breadsticks and a cup of black coffee waited for him on his desk as a reward for slipping into his office without seeing his secretary or his secretary's secretary.

Cardinal Killane was a tall man. His narrow forehead was scalloped by curved temples and his pink skin was only a little sullied by liver spots. His long hands were still strong and he could walk into the ground any priest in the archdiocese. On a less complicated man his blue eyes would have been called twinkling. But people like to look into twinkling eyes, and he noticed a great number of people looked away from his. Not the people he cared about, though. It was the sort of judgment he never would have indulged himself in when he was younger. Or was it adversity that brought out this asperity, he asked himself.

His creation as cardinal of the Apostolic See of New York was not universally popular. He'd started out right, an Irish boy from Boston's Brighton neighborhood. Never mind that his father was a devout atheist—a lot of good Irishmen were. Graduated Fordham University, highest honors, class of 1929. Ordained after much soul searching about his vanity in the spring of 1933. He wanted to stay in the city and work with those crushed by the Depression, but his superiors saw in him the beginnings of a messiah complex and they sent him instead to the British West Indies, which for reasons of access fell into the New York diocese. There he helped Trinidad blacks against the British and developed a messiah complex that was truly colossal.

Father Killane was a problem, and the then-Cardinal Hayes decided on the traditional answer to overly bright and aggressive priests: Rome. There Killane entered the Vatican's American College with an assigned curriculum of Asian studies, a regimen designed to increase his humility. With perverse pleasure, Killane took to the subject, going from the college to a minor position in the Vatican archives where he collated centuries-old reports from long-dead missionaries. He might have continued in that library for the rest of his life metamorphosed into an actual bookworm, he thought, while Italy and the rest of the world were shot to hell. It wasn't to be. As the war against the Japanese drew to an end, France began reorganizing its Indochina empire and it sought Vatican aid, because the French colonial records had been destroyed. A forty-year-old American priest with not only a command of French and the major Indochinese languages but also a superb memory of the religious and political alliances of the region was dispatched on the first plane for Hanoi. Killane served two years traveling through Vietnam, Laos and Cambodia, and the reports he turned in were almost uniformly pessimistic. Which was why, on his return to the Vatican, his superiors were surprised by a new request that the archivist be lent to the French command in Algeria.

The Vatican Secretariat of State felt it should have the benefit of Killane's talents. After a year's training in the

Curia office, he went as assistant to the apostolic nuncio in Japan, conducting clandestine arrangements for the protection of millions of Catholics left in Communist China. When the Korean War wrecked those arrangements, Killane was not blamed the way a secular diplomat might have been. He was created a monsignor and appointed assistant to the nuncio to Germany. From there he worked his way up through the levels of the secretariat, consecrated titular bishop of Tagaste and, later, titular bishop of Zeugma. At last, he became first assistant to the Secretary of State, the first American that close to control of the church's foreign policy. The reason, he knew, was that in reality he was so little American. In the past thirty-five years he'd only been home six times. Neither Cardinal Hayes nor any of the other men who exiled their problem to Rome was still alive. He'd spoken half a dozen languages more often than English. His work and life lay in the Vatican.

All that ended with his sudden elevation to the College of Cardinals. His agile mind worked it out quickly enough when the shock was past. The two main contenders for the red biretta were New York bishops who had so skilfully drawn support from the other American cardinals that the appointment of either would offend half the American hierarchy. They'd looked around for an uninvolved American bishop of Irish descent and they'd found John Killane. So, only as a compromise solution, the new cardinal came home.

He took a pocket watch from his cassock, pulled a pair of gold legs from its back and set it in the middle of his desk. The minute ticking of the watch reminded him that his secretary would appear no sooner than thirty seconds and no later than fifty.

His cathedral administrator and secretary, Monsignor Burns, was among those who referred to the cardinal as the Italian. They didn't let Killane's name fool them. He was nothing like the honest shepherds who had gone before. Away from the United States, the cardinal had forgotten the fierce Irish Catholic prejudice against their Italian brothers, whom they regarded as subpagans incapable of taking religion seriously. Of the nine American cardinals, eight were Irish and none were Italian. If Saint Peter were Irish, there would be precious few Italians in Heaven.

"Good morning, Your Eminence. Sleep well?" Monsignor Burns asked as he entered with the morning mail.

Roman and Isadore moved slowly through the rush-hour traffic. As usual, the cars on Park Avenue reminded Roman of ants moving through a cemetery. Being in one of them only added to his bad temper.

"The captain pulled your file a week ago, but he's always doing that," Isadore told him.

He turned right at Forty-Ninth Street and again at Madison. Rockefeller Center swung into view and out behind the spires of St. Patrick's. Isadore cautiously turned into the courtyard of a Renaissance manor in brownstone. The other cars displayed CLERGY plaques in their rear windows or bumper decals saying SOCIETY FOR THE PROPAGATION OF THE FAITH. Over the main façade were two colorful shields and in gilt ARCHDIOCESE OF NEW YORK.

"I swear I don't know any more than you do," Isadore repeated.

A priest who didn't look old enough to be out of high school emerged from the main building and ran over to the car.

"Are you Mr. Grey?" he asked Isadore. Isadore pointed to Roman. "You're Mr. Grey. I'm Father Young," he said a trifle defensively. "Come with me."

"He goes too." Roman pointed back at Isadore.

"Police?" The priest gave Isadore a skeptical examination. "All right, you can come too, but hurry."

They got out of the car and Father Young led them across Madison with a maximum of bustling.

"You must refer to him as Your Eminence," he instructed his flock.

"Refer to whom as Your Eminence?" Roman asked.

"Cardinal Killane," the priest responded with adolescent satisfaction.

St. Patrick's took up nearly the whole block between Fiftieth and Fifty-first streets, but set on each corner on Madison were three-story houses that were imitations of the cathedral in the same white marble, *petits fours* next to a wedding cake. Father Young opened the front door of the house on Fiftieth Street for the Gypsy's reluctant foot.

On the foyer walls were portraits of past cardinals and archbishops looking out from their harnesses of red satin and white lace. Young hurried Roman along.

"You've got the wrong Grey," Roman told the priest.

"That's what they all say," Isadore whispered.

As they waited outside an office door, Young gave the detective and the Gypsy a last review. If he didn't have the right Mr. Grey, it was too late now. He brushed a piece of lint from Isadore's lapel.

"Remember, it's 'Your Eminence.' "

The door was opened by a priest, and they entered a high-ceilinged room with no more adornment than a crucifix and a picture of the Holy Father. A big man in a business suit sat to the side in one of the room's throne-back chairs. The man seated behind the desk was in black, with the short red cape of the Prince of the Church.

Father Young introduced them. "Mr. Grey, Your Eminence."

"We've already met," Roman said.

Young and Isadore were shocked. Killane smiled.

"Thank you, father, that will be all."

As Young left he shot Roman a murderous glance for mislaying his only instruction.

"It was John Killigan yesterday," Roman pointed out when the door had closed.

"Yes, I'm afraid it was," Killane apologized. "This is my secretary, Monsignor Burns. And Captain Reggel."

Reggel, the big man sitting down, made a bow from his chair. He had small, dark eyes, heavy cheekbones and white-blond hair. His sharply cut suit revealed an athletic body that had thickened without going to fat.

"This is Detective Sergeant Isadore," Roman said.

Isadore, who had hoped to go unnoticed, found himself making his own awkward bow.

"Will you have a seat, please?" the cardinal asked.

The detective sat.

"I can tell you're irritated with all this, Mr. Grey," the cardinal went on, "and I don't blame you. But we didn't come to a decision until last night."

"Your Eminence has good reasons, I'm sure—"

"Please." Killane put his hand up. "Before you think about leaving, what do you know about the Holy Crown of Hungary?"

Roman sat down. Isadore noticed him taking more interest in the man called Reggel. The Gypsy's fingers touched his chin once, the first nervous gesture Isadore ever saw him make.

"I've never seen it," Roman said lightly.

"The Holy Crown is the most important crown jewel in the world," Burns reprimanded him. "It is also one of the Catholic Church's most valuable relics. It was sent to Saint Stephen when he became the first Christian King of Hungary in the year 1000 by Pope Sylvester II. Up to that point the Magyar tribes, of which Stephen was leader, were pagan.

"However, at the end of World War Two, when the Russians were approaching Budapest, the Nazi-supported government attempted to send the crown to Switzerland. Fortunately, Hungarian soldiers serving the Wehrmacht took the crown to Salzburg instead and gave it to the American Army. As with the rest of what the Nazis stole, we intended to turn the Holy Crown back to its lawful owner, the Hungarian nation in this case. Which would have happened if a Communist regime hadn't taken over. We have held the crown in trust for the Hungarian people in Washington since then."

"Is that close enough?" Killane asked Roman.

"It sounds good."

"He likes Gauloises. Did you bring them?" Killane asked the monsignor.

"Yes, of course."

Burns set a stand-up ashtray beside Roman's chair and took a baby-blue pack of cigarettes out of his cassock and offered them to him.

"No, thanks, I have my own."

Killane waited until Roman lit up.

"In Washington until now," the cardinal continued. "This afternoon it's being announced"—he took the monsignor's pack and lit one for himself—"being announced in Washington and Budapest that we're giving the Holy Crown

back. It'll return in time for the anniversary of Saint
Stephen's death this fall. You know, you don't look terribly
surprised."

He isn't, Isadore thought and got his first pleasure out
of a confusing morning.

"Well, Your Eminence," Roman was saying diplomati-
cally, "after meeting a cardinal like yourself, it's hard to be
surprised by anything."

"You must be wondering what this has to do with you,
or us."

"I am."

Isadore felt the cardinal's eyes flick over him once with
the cold sweep of a camera.

"As I told you yesterday, your name came up as a con-
sultant. Apparently, some of the jewelry houses and private
collectors in the city value your opinion on crown jewelry.
And different odds and ends that come into your hands."
He paused. "That's not the way the police put it, inci-
dentally. You'll pardon the extent of my inquiries, but
they were absolutely essential."

"I deal mostly in antiques."

"Of course, but you have the qualifications."

"For what?"

"You see, it was the American State Department's idea
to whip up enthusiasm for the crown's return before Congress could get it in its head it was rash appeasement. The
department did too good a job, perhaps. One of the Con-
gressmen from New York, a Representative Szemely, demanded that Hungarian-Americans have a chance to look
at this famous crown. It's quite an issue with them. To
keep Szemely and Congress happy it's been decided to display the Holy Crown before its return. It's true that once
the crown is in Budapest Americans aren't likely to get near
it again.

"The display was going to be held at the Metropolitan
Museum, because, you see, there are more Hungarians here
than in Washington. Our friends in Budapest were upset, on
the other hand, since a museum display would reduce their
national symbol to a feature in a sideshow. The church was
none too happy either over the secular treatment of such
a sacred relic."

"St. Patrick's," Isadore said.

"Precisely." Killane gave him a nod of approval. "In our St. Patrick's. Arriving in a week to be displayed from Monday to Friday in the sanctuary before the high altar. At night it will be taken underneath the sanctuary to the sacristy. And when it arrives we will need someone to examine it and, while it is in our custody, to look after it. I want you to do it for me, Mr. Grey."

Seeing the request coming for ten minutes didn't help. Roman still refused to believe it.

"There are hundreds of registered jewelers better suited. I could name you twenty right now."

"I know their names. There are other qualifications besides being expert on medieval crowns. The man we have must be Catholic. That narrows the field significantly. He must speak fluent Hungarian, as he will be working with a Hungarian expert and there can be no misunderstanding. The field becomes very narrow. And our man must not be identified with any émigré or royalist associations. That, Mr. Grey, narrows the field down to you. You are what is called a compromise solution, and if it makes you feel any better, you have my sympathy. You are the only choice."

Roman shook his head.

"I can't believe you spoke to the police for very long, Your Eminence. To be blunt, they would tell you I'd take the crown and run."

"They had a number of misgivings. But, to be equally blunt, you won't have the opportunity to abscond with the jewels. The crown will be under police guard all the time. And, frankly, I have some confidence in my judgment."

The room fell silent until Roman turned to the one man who hadn't said a word.

"Reggel *ur,* how do you feel about having a *cigany* looking after the Holy Crown?"

The Hungarian smiled broadly. His English was faintly slurred.

"Gypsies and Magyars always recognize each other, don't they?"

"Like Germans and Jews," Roman agreed.

Reggel's smile didn't slip.

"The cardinal has explained the situation," he said. "I am willing to comply with it, as I will be in charge of security."

"Captain Reggel is chief of security for the Hungarian mission to the United Nations," Killane explained.

"I bet he is," Roman agreed. "Thank you very much for your interest, Your Eminence, but I told you before there was a trip I had to make. I'm sorry, you'll have to excuse me."

Outside in the courtyard, Isadore asked Roman why he couldn't put off his trip for two weeks.

"Because I might not go then. And then where would I be?"

Isadore understood the Gypsy meant something worse than New York City.

CHAPTER
6

ALTHOUGH NEW YORK is called Rommeville by American Gypsies, it has never had a fixed Gypsy community like European cities. Paris police files, for example, trace one family of the Kalderash tribe through 400 years from its first arrival in the Cour des Miracles. Today, surrounded by Algerians and Vietnamese on the Right Bank, the Kalderash continue their venerable trades as coppersmiths and thieves—and the police files continue to swell like a family Bible.

The Spanish police of Granada have a simpler task since they have no intention of making arrests. Their Gitanos have always lived on the Sacro Monte under the eye of the Alhambra. Unless a tourist is knifed or the Gypsy-hating Guardia Civil finds an excuse to storm the hill, its inhabitants are left strictly alone. Granada's tourist trade is built on the flamenco music of its Gypsies.

Rommeville is different. Its shape has constantly grown and changed, pushing Gypsy camps from the hills of Harlem to the farms of Brooklyn and Queens. When Rommeville became a megalopolis a new sort of wilderness appeared in its heart, and the Gypsies, ever opportunists, flowed into the vacuum.

Part of the vacuum was an abandoned apartment building off Houston Street in the lower half of Manhattan—abandoned but not vacant, for the Gypsies had moved in.

"Us or the crazy dope addicts," the Pivli Petulengro told Roman. "We pay the police and they say they're happy we're here."

"We tried some of the condemned buildings in the Bronx," John Petulengro said. "They were in terrible condition."

"No better than Europe," his grandmother agreed. She was called the Pivli, the Widow, because despite a mouthful of gold teeth it was unlikely she'd marry again.

They were in the building's lobby, a drafty affair of rose marble and broken mirrors. Families of Rom filed past them carrying shopping bags of food and drink. There were two elevators that didn't work and a side room where tenants once collected their mail and which the Petulengro brothers used for storing hubcaps.

"I am very happy my boys are going with you," the Pivli told Roman as they moved out of the way of a group of musicians with violins. "You are a Rom of great respect."

"Thank you," Roman said gravely. To show embarrassment would have been bad taste. If a Gypsy couldn't take a compliment, who could?

"They'll learn a lot from you."

"I hope so." He cast a resigned eye on the hubcap collection.

"I just wish I could go." She sighed like a girl.

The lobby was dominated by a Cadillac parked in the middle of it. Inside the car, *chals* climbed over the seats and played with a snake's nest of wires. One of the boys finally matched a wire and a loud honk erupted. Kore squirmed out from under the car. A red welt sat in the middle of the grease on his forehead.

"You have worms for fingers," he yelled at the boys. "I told you to wait. Now I'm going to cut your fingers off and feed them to the fish."

Kore noticed Roman and the Pivli. He touched his forehead and looked at the lack of blood on his finger. Shrugging, he nonchalantly cleaned his ear with the same finger.

"Good boys, actually. I was just joking."

The boys weren't so sure. They locked the car doors.

"At least they got you out. I've been looking all over for you," Roman told him.

"I've been here all the time." He gestured to the car. "What do you think?"

Roman made a tour of the Cadillac. When he got back, he shook Kore's hand again.

"*Rom san tu!* How did you get this monster of a *mobile* in here?"

"Drove it in, how else? The boards broke coming up the stairs, though. That made a noise, I'll tell you! I've been fixing the axle ever since, when the *chals*. . . ." Kore glanced back at the car. It was empty. The boys had used their opportunity to escape.

"It's ready now?"

"What is this, a restaurant or a lobby?" Kore snarled at a passing musician. "You almost put your fiddle through my window. How can a man get any work done around here? Of course, it's ready," he added to Roman.

The car had no hood and the huge engine gleamed with polished chrome. Kore hot-wired the battery and the car came to life.

"Listen."

He handed Roman a plastic tube and placed the other end over a cylinder. A throaty purr lowered to a whisper as Kore depressed the carburetor lever. No factory-ground pistons hummed as sweetly as the product of Kore's skill. When he lifted the lever the lobby reverberated.

"It's beautiful."

"You can't buy a car like this," Kore said, pleased with Roman's enthusiasm.

Roman wasn't finished, though. He searched the engine block until he found the vehicle identification number, then opened the door to check the VIN on the dash. They both looked like originals, but they didn't match.

"Well, that's the last one," Kore protested. "I've already done the numbers on the transmission and the chassis. Don't worry; when it comes to stamping numbers, I am a

Kalderash goldsmith. Everything is taken care of. Look."
Kore leaned into the car and took a stack of papers from
the glove compartment. Roman recognized a Motor Ve-
hicle-50 form on top.

"Racki and I went into a showroom to see the new
models. The manager was going to throw us out until I
shook some money at him, and then, of course, he took me
into his office to buy a *mobile* right away. Well, greed is a
sad thing, the man couldn't think straight. His office had
glass walls, so he could see Racki going from car to car,
getting behind the wheel, you know. He notices Racki is
scratching a little bit as if he has, you know, some sort of
problem. He wants to sell me this car so he doesn't say
anything, but all he can see is Racki scratching here and
there as if the *chal* has bugs by the *kumpania*. And finally
the manager remembers that he has to get in his cars afterward. He jumps up and runs out yelling. Naturally, I am
insulted and leave, but not before I've been in his desk and
chor five of these ownership forms, one for myself and
four for my friends. Notice that I did not allow selfishness to overcome me."

"You certainly didn't. You have me down here as the
owner."

"Do I?" Kore seemed surprised.

"Never mind. What else have you got?"

Kore quickly showed Roman a pair of Canadian passports. Paper-clipped to the front of one was a picture of
John Petulengro.

"What *nav gajikanes* did you give him?"

"See for yourself."

"Of course," Roman laughed. "John Smith."

Kore nodded proudly and then drew Roman off to a
side of the lobby. Although there was no one in earshot,
for once he spoke quietly.

"Romano, there's something I have to say. You know
that with me it has always been *Rom Romesa, Gajo Gajesa.*
But if you are determined to bring this girl along, it's all
right with me. I'm ashamed of the way I acted at your
apartment the other night. I don't have any excuse. Do
you forgive me?"

"Easily." A lot more easily, Roman knew, than it was

for Kore to break one of his firmest laws. "Come on, before we start crying, let's go down to the party."

"*Rom san tu,* Romano!"

"I'm glad you're getting the idea."

They started for the basement door arm in arm.

"Romano, come here!"

Standing in the entrance of the lobby was Celie Miyeyeshti and one of the two small girls who always attended her.

"Come with us to the party," Roman invited her. "I've never felt like a party more than tonight."

"Forget the party. Come now."

Kore stood aside.

Celie was a witch, if witches are women who can rule without money or sex. There were around the world matriarchs who knew more of the race's unwritten history and laws than anyone else, and she was one of them. The King of the Gypsies was a pale fiction next to the immense fact of Celie Miyeyeshti.

"All right. Drink some for me," Roman told Kore.

She led the way to her black Fleetwood limousine. The night air was balmy and every jackhammer, bus engine and sanitation truck in the city seemed to have ceased the moment before.

Celie, enormous with necklaces of gold coins and a volume of red petticoats, took up the back seat with just enough room left over for her two small attendants. A man Roman didn't know sat on a jump seat. As soon as Roman pulled up the other, Celie's car began moving.

"What do you know about Saint Stephen's Crown?" she asked.

Besides being very old and very fat, her face was charged with energy, and Celie overwhelmed the others in the car like a sun among planets.

"Everyone is asking that question."

"I'm asking it now."

Evasiveness might do for priests; it wouldn't with Celie. He told her about his visit to the cardinal's office.

"Why you?"

"They had some reasons that weren't good enough. Besides, I'm leaving in a few days."

"You're not leaving," Celie said before he was even finished speaking.

Roman sat back on the jump seat as well as he could. They swayed as the car went around the corner, but his eyes never left hers.

"Does this have anything to do with the *gaji?*"

A gloaming streetlight passed over Celie's face but he read nothing except resignation.

"Don't I know you too well for that?" She dismissed his question and touched the knee of the other Rom. "This is Punka Lovell. He came here tonight from Royal Town because he has something to tell you."

Royal Town was London. Punka was short even for the Lovell clan, and he spoke in the round dialect of the English Rom, calling *"gaja"* gorgio.

"We got a call today from friends in Vienna. They said the Department of Minorities is going to take all the *chals.*"

"Where? What Department of Minorities?"

"In Hungary. Take all Gypsy children to special schools to solve the minority problem. The *kapos* of the Rom were taken to the department last night and told. But the chief *kapo* was told in private that the order wasn't final if they could influence a Rom here to do a favor for them. He was talking about you and the Holy Crown."

"It's insane. Why threaten thousands so one Rom here would look at a crown? Only a fanatic would do that. What makes you so important?"

"Romano is an important man," Celie said stiffly. "There are times when I have my doubts, but someday he will prove it. Romano, what do you think of this?"

"It's a bluff. A madman's bluff."

"You know the man?"

"We met in the cardinal's home. His name is Reggel."

The car cruised north on the East River Drive.

"You could tell the cardinal then," Celie suggested.

Roman knew it wasn't the sort of suggestion she would have made if she thought he'd take it. He had no more control over his decision than over the plunging car.

"I'll tell him I'll take care of the crown."

"Boona," Punka cried.

The English Rom's eyes smudged with tears of relief.

All Roman could see on Celie's face and on the faces of the two small girls was satisfaction.

The car stopped and let Roman out. By now he knew the car had been moving toward Kennedy for Punka to carry his answer back. As if there were more than one answer. Punka waved out the window as the car pulled away. Celie never looked back.

Captain Ferenc Reggel followed the flashlight of Congressman Imre Szemely into a playground between Seventy-seventh and Seventy-eighth streets. The Congressman played the beam over the walls and up the basketball backboard. The net was ripped off, and written over the hoop was SPORTS IS A RIP OFF.

"You see, even here," Szemely said.

They walked the length of the court to the back door of a store facing First Avenue. Szemely unlocked it and they went in. Glossy black sausages were strung out on enamel tables below racks of spiced hams. One wall was stained red from the bright tempura of rose paprika. A man sat at a table waiting for them, the overhead light catching the white bristle over his chin and hollowed cheeks. As Reggel and Szemely approached, he removed his steel-rimmed glasses but did not stand.

"Doktor Martinovics, Kapitany Reggel," Szemely introduced them.

The Congressman was nervous despite the fact the meeting was taking place in his store. He fumbled around the cabinets looking for glasses and an ashtray. The other two men ignored him.

"I remember you," the doctor told Reggel. "Your father and I were friends—did you know that? That was when he was in the Royal Guards."

"That was a very long time ago," Reggel answered with the accent on "very."

"I've seen you since. I left for the last time in fifty-six, remember?"

Reggel didn't need the reminder that Martinovics was one of the last to escape Budapest. In New York the doctor of philosophy had become head of the largest Freedom Fighter organization. Other Hungarian émigré groups existed, but Martinovics' was the one that hadn't succumbed to self-pity and paranoia. It did so by keeping its hate for the Communist regime pure and sharp. Szemely was the elected representative of the Seventeenth Congressional District, but he was the doctor's surrogate, and Martinovics' influence was just as great in Chicago, St. Louis, Cleveland and Los Angeles.

"Why did you ask to see me?" Martinovics asked Reggel.

"The Holy Crown."

"Ah, yes." He took the bottle Szemely had found, poured out two glasses of golden Tokay and pushed one to Reggel. "I have heard something about it recently."

"Why did you have Szemely demand a show of the crown here?" Reggel asked. "You could have stopped its return or just let it go. So why this?"

"This is democracy," Martinovics informed Reggel. "Representative Szemely can do whatever he likes."

The store owner nodded in servile agreement.

"I want to know what you plan when the crown is on display. A disruption to embarrass everyone? Even steal it? If you want to protest, to walk about with signs, go right ahead. Only be warned that if I ever see the crown in danger I will protect it any way I see fit."

"My friend's son, once the crown is in your hands it is already in danger. We would be the ones rescuing it, not you. There is a rumor going around that you plan to melt the Holy Crown down."

"Do you think that, doctor?"

Martinovics winced in disgust. "It's a very unhappy thing that exile does to one's friends. You would think they were talking about China instead of Hungary sometimes. At any rate, why should I be telling the Communist policeman about our plans? I fail to understand why you come at this late hour with threats."

"No threats, doctor. I come with an appeal. Don't show the world Hungarians fighting like animals over the Holy Crown. Anything else, but leave this alone. I am a Socialist officer and you are an émigré. So be it, but we are both Magyars first. Your first duty is to the preservation of Saint Stephen's Crown as the symbol of Hungary, not to endanger or humiliate it with political quarrels. If you love your country you will not do it."

"I am not in love with the government you want to take it to."

"No matter what government, it is still Hungary," Reggel almost shouted. He continued in a lower voice. "It will no longer be a hostage on foreign soil but back where it belongs. In time all governments change." He waved aside the start of Martinovics' objections. "What it changes to I don't know and I don't care. Marxist, Fascist—so what?"

"A great deal." The doctor shoved his chair back and stood up. "I care what happens. The men who died with me in Budapest, they cared. It's traitors like you who don't. You have the country and now you want the crown so that the regime can clutch it to its breasts and say, 'Yes, this proves beyond any doubt, we are truly the legitimate heirs of Hungary.' Well, Reggel *ur,* we may not count for much in Hungary, but as long as the Holy Crown remains here we can put a stop to that last farce."

The whites of Martinovics' eyes were yellowed and flecked with blood. His suit, once custom tailored, hung on a body shrunk with age. Reggel sensed the despair of a man whose body had started to betray him and filed the fact away for another day.

"You see, I remember you very well, captain. Even to the boy who led the procession to the Basilica on Saint Stephen's Day, you with your prayer book and the girls with their bouquets. How soon was that before you were getting whores for the Wehrmacht? Now you kill for the Russians while better men have to die here a thousand miles from home."

Szemely turned his face away and rested his hands on a sweaty coil of sausage. Reggel listened unmoved. He'd expected nothing less from Martinovics than the most violent denunciation. Szemely was uncomfortable because he was Americanized.

The doctor's harangue lasted a full ten minutes, and at the end of it he sat down to wet his mouth.

"Will you leave the Holy Crown alone, though?" Reggel asked.

The old man glanced from his anxious cohort to the

unruffled security officer. A wry smile broke through the
grizzle of his lips.

"I could have some men here in a minute who would
not leave you alone," he told Reggel.

"The crown."

"You dare." Martinovics sighed in awe. "You dare to
plead with me."

"Let me put it another way then. I order you." Reggel
spoke so softly he had to repeat his words.

"How could Captain Reggel order me?"

It took an hour for Reggel to explain to the doctor and
prove it beyond the old man's most desperate disbelief. It
was Reggel's only card but a trump and once played assured
success. At two in the morning Reggel left by the back door
for the playground and the street.

"One thing," Martinovics called out.

Reggel stopped, turning around. The doctor was framed
in the doorway, a silhouette except for the light around the
steel frames of his glasses. Reggel, having won, listened
with the mildest of interest.

"If you ever return to me, Magyar, consider yourself
dead."

As Martinovics moved back into the room's light his
face seemed more hollow than before, the hand on the
door jamb like lines of chalk. Then the door closed.

CHAPTER
7.

ROMAN PUT HIS hands on the window and leaned toward the river. On the far bank a utility plant loosed deceptively white puffs of smoke into the sky. She'd been asleep when he came home and gone when he woke up, so he hadn't told Dany yet that they weren't going. The wind tugged the puffs free of their giant stacks and carried them like orphans to the sea.

Breakfast was meat fried with garlic and onions. He took the pan and a fork with him back to the window and watched again while he ate.

Toothpaste turned the garlic sour and he cut himself shaving. His body was nearly hairless, but he had a beard that dulled one razor blade a day. When he was dressed he gave the nick a last look in the mirror, avoiding his eyes. Before leaving, he removed his tie and exchanged his suit coat for a leather jacket.

On the street nothing changed. The same neighbor walking the same brace of clipped white poodles was at the corner. Her coat was white with rings of white fur and raised the usual grim possibility in his mind. She smiled at him because he always seemed happy to see her.

45

He found Kore in a garage. A dozen Gypsies stood around while two others carved stolen cars with acetylene torches. Kore sat disconsolately on an oil drum.

"You heard."

Kore nodded. His clothes seemed more battered than ever.

"It's only another week," Roman pointed out as much for his own sake as Kore's.

A torch's blue-and-white flame burned through the fender of a Jaguar. The fender fell on a waiting blanket. On the ground in an unrolled pack were the tools of the trade: the lock drill called a slapper, hooks for passing through windows to lift locks and rings of manufacturers' master keys. A *gaja* dealer arrived and stood on the side without a welcome. He stared at Roman, who was immaculate in contrast to the other Gypsies.

"There are too many complications around you, Romano," Kore observed at last. "With every light another color."

Serious Romany was a language of metaphors and Kore was very serious.

"A man can ride two horses only so long. Each day I see you are more with them than us. First the girl and then the police. Maybe you want to be the first Gypsy in their heaven?"

Enviously Roman watched the men dismantling the sports car. Even in their iron masks they followed tradition. For hundreds of years nobles commissioned Gypsies to "buy" horses for them, then asked in what direction it would be unwise to ride. There hadn't been many Gypsy antique dealers.

"Give me another week, Kore. Then I'll be free."

Kore's eyes showed skepticism but he softened.

"I hear you're working with Hungarians. I can get you a gun." He gestured at the car dealer.

"No, thanks."

"I forget. You don't even carry a proper knife."

Kore raised his hands. There was nothing more he could do.

"What are you going to do?" one of the Gypsies asked when Roman was gone.

Kore raised his hands again with frustration. "I'll wait."

The car Odrich rented was a Chrysler Charger. He drove it to a garage rented beforehand by one of his men, a tall blond named Karl. Karl was waiting, dressed in work coveralls.

When the garage door closed behind him, Odrich turned on the headlights. On each side of the grille, panels rolled up to reveal the lights. Odrich turned off the ignition.

"It's best to take the spring out entirely," he said. "We can tape the crown in."

Phillips screws collected in Karl's hand as he worked on the left headlight. Once it was loose he pulled it out to hang by its wires over the bumper.

"And from the car to the church, Papa?" he asked. "Have you resolved that yet?"

"Yes. That antique dealer stays on my mind and it came to me while I was thinking of him, so at least he's served us that purpose. We use a perfectly simple method. The crown goes underwater."

"You should have told me about the cardinal right away. I'm very proud."

"Good. I hope I didn't lose you any jobs you could have had this week."

"The photographers are getting disgusted with me. Too sexy for the Henri Bendel spread, they said. But how old can you be and still wear Mary Janes?"

"I wish I knew."

Half the apartment's furniture was in storage and there was nothing left in the bedroom but the bed he was on and the vanity bureau Dany sat at. She was naked, brushing her freshly washed hair before the mirror.

"Would you like it if I had a beauty mark?" she asked. "Do *chis* have beauty marks?"

Roman sat up and watched, admiring the live curves of her body half hidden by the long fall of brown hair. Each stroke took forever.

He got off the bed and walked to the table, standing behind Dany.

"You want a beauty mark?"

"If you think I should."

He looked at her reflection in the mirror. Her face had broadened and become more beautiful in the time he'd known her, the childish model he first met nearly disappeared. One or two strands of hair hung over her breasts and she brushed the hair out of the way.

"*Chis* don't have beauty marks. If you want to, you can put blue dots on the inside and outside of each eye. That's to keep away the Evil Eye."

She leaned toward the mirror and considered it. Her pupils were blue and brown, mixed like shards of glass.

"The dots would bring out the blue in them," she said. "What do Roms wear to avoid the Evil Eye?"

"They wear one earring."

"You don't."

"My father didn't either. Maybe he should have."

"Tell me about your father. You never say anything about him."

She put the brush down and looked up at him in the mirror.

"I'll tell you one thing. He used to brush my mother's hair. I used to sit in a corner of the wagon and watch them and listen to them talk." He picked up the brush. "She had long black hair and it shined."

He put the brush on the side of her head and pulled it down, sweeping it through Dany's hair. She sat very still, feeling the soft, deliberate tug of the bristles.

"I'll tell you something else about my father," Roman went on. "Something that happened before the last trip to Rumania. We were in England and it happened to be a bad time. Our *kumpania* had lost some wagons in a snowstorm, and we couldn't stop to rest because the police kept moving us from one council ground to another.

"There was too much snow on the ground for any *gaja* to come have their fortunes told. We had no money and no food, so my father and I went into the woods to shoot something. The police were waiting, of course, and as soon as we set foot in the forest they stopped us and took my father's rifle away. That was so we couldn't poach any of the game the landlord wanted for his shooting season."

Dany watched as he spoke and continued rhythmically to brush her hair. There was something ridiculous about the way his muscles strained to brush as gently as possible, but she didn't say anything because she was afraid of breaking the spell.

"I was angry enough to cry. We needed food to eat and they were saving it for the landlord's sport. But my father handed his rifle over and we turned away as if it didn't matter.

"It started to snow again. Heavily. My father ripped his kerchief in two and we stuffed it into the bottom of my shoes. We trudged on through the woods, and I knew that we weren't returning to camp until we had something to bring. The snow came up to my knees and my father asked if I wanted to go back. I said no, and we went on."

Dany could picture the five-year-old Roman refusing. The brush hissed through her hair.

"Finally, we came to a meadow. The snow was high and very bright. My father went first, and I followed in his trail as well as I could. When we were far out in the meadow, we stopped and sat down. My father sat down first so I could sit in his lap.

"We must have been there an hour without talking, just watching the snow fall, before we saw the rabbit. It had its white coat on and sometimes you couldn't see it when it wasn't moving. At least I couldn't. I'm sure my father could.

" '*Kamas shooshi?*' he asked me.

" 'Yes,' I said, 'I like rabbit.'

"We stood up, and so did the rabbit when he saw us, freezing the way they do before they run. The three of us stayed like that, waiting for the other to move, and my father began to whistle. It was a simple *czardas*, and he whistled it over and over again. Sometimes I thought the rabbit had run away when I couldn't see him through the snow, but he was still there. My father took off his jacket very slowly and held it out to the rabbit. Then he put it on the snow. He walked away, still whistling, and the rabbit, instead of running away, stayed where he was and watched the jacket. My father walked around in a great circle, and never once did the rabbit look away from the whistling jacket. He was still watching it when my father grabbed him from behind and killed him.

"We had a very nice supper."

The brush, which had stopped, began moving through her hair again.

"Did your father ever teach you how to do it?"

"The Nazis killed him in the spring," Roman reported matter-of-factly.

"I suppose it wouldn't do you much good in a city anyway."

Roman didn't answer until he was satisfied with his work and he put the brush on the table.

"Maybe it helps. Have you ever heard a crown whistle?"

Dany shook her head. "Is that another Romany trick?"

"Not Romany. I don't know what it is."

Dany wanted to ask him about his mother but she knew he wouldn't reveal anything more about his parents tonight. She stood up, moving to him and putting her arms around his back.

"I love you."

"*Mande cam tute.*"

With that, they went to bed.

FRISS

CHAPTER
8

A GOTHIC CATHEDRAL is designed to miniaturize the body and elevate the soul. The effect on Isadore as he came through the doors of St. Patrick's was one of dizziness. He'd been in small churches on police business before, but he'd never been in a full cathedral and nothing in the world like St. Patrick's. He was no carping critic, and he was stunned.

A synagogue had straight, logical lines, and God was content to remain an Omnipotent One. Here the vaults soared, slender ribs spreading and intersecting like the lines of a curved universe. In between stone columns, God divided and subdivided into a merry-go-round of martyrs and saints. The air itself was animated with colors from stained glass. Fifth Avenue was farther away than the distance of a door. He seized on the sight of the commissioner and two detectives standing in the sanctuary.

Commissioner Jack Lynch waited grimly. He was Black Irish, short and aggressive, thirty years a cop and only five months head of the New York Police Department. The day after his appointment reporters asked if he was going to clean up the city, and he said that was like trying to stop venereal disease by changing the sheets. Since then the mayor had kept him on a tight rein.

"Sir, I'd like to make a protest," were Isadore's first words. "I have two cases coming up in court."

"Sergeant, I have two hundred thousand cases in court. I have a thousand murders, ten thousand rapes, ten times that many violent crimes. Do I have time to worry about your problems?"

"It's just that I don't think I'm the right man."

Lynch paced the gray and green terrazzo.

"Of course, you're not. No one said you were. But thanks to your files, we picked out an expert with a record and the expert says he won't do the job unless you handle our end. Don't you know it's easier to switch detectives than it is experts?"

Isadore said nothing. Neither yes nor no seemed quite right.

"Today I had to pull a very good cop, Lieutenant Donnelly, a Knight of Columbus, and put you in his place. Which means that with a city seething in crime I have to come here and talk to the cardinal about some crown I don't give a—" He tapped his foot and let the thought drop. "I told the mayor you were a competent man."

"Thank you."

"Why? What else could I say? That I put the department mystery man in charge of this political circus? That you may still be a sergeant at forty-nine but you deliver a lovely lecture on Gypsies at City College?"

"Nothing so strange about that," Isadore muttered.

The commissioner gave him another glare as he paced by.

"I don't want any Kosygin incidents with these Freedom Fighters. BOSSI will give you a rundown on their organizations. Don't worry about the transfer from the airport. Donnelly will take care of that. You just handle the church. I'm giving you ten men. St. Patrick's holds five thousand. Think you'll be able to screen them? Don't start shaking your head until I'm finished talking, please. The Hungarian captain brings in ten men, too."

Isadore had a thought. "Maybe the Hungarian won't like the idea of me coming in this late."

"Why not? Before, he had to share the command with a lieutenant; now he can order a sergeant around. Anything wrong with that?"

"No," Isadore heard himself saying.

"Good. I suppose you'll know how to get along with him. Cooperative but not obsequious." Lynch looked at Isadore sadly. "Call me personally if anything happens. Good luck."

Isadore thought the commissioner was going to shake his hand, but Lynch turned to the altar, crossed himself and walked off.

Isadore knew the two detectives who had kept silent up to this point. One was president of the Emerald Society, an association comprised of the forty percent of the police force who were Irish. The other was chief of detectives and president of Shinrom, the department's Jewish society.

"You really did it this time, Harry," the latter said. "I guess we should just be happy the Jewish Defense League isn't involved in this."

"Al," Isadore began, but the man was already leaving to join the commissioner.

The other man patted Isadore's shoulder.

"Don't take it so hard, sergeant. You know Chief Meyer, always in a sweat about something. And Jack . . . well, you know it's even tougher for a good cop to be commissioner. I'll calm them down and if any cop on the squad gives you trouble, you just tell them you're okay with Captain Gleason. Right?"

"I appreciate that, captain."

After the two men shook hands the lieutenant crossed himself and went down the sanctuary steps. At the communion rail he stopped.

"But, Jesus," he winced. "A Gypsy and a Jew guarding St. Patrick's Cathedral."

Reggel watched Isadore from above on the triforium gallery. The round sergeant would present no difficulties, he felt. The man was intelligent but definitely not shrewd. To begin with, the sergeant trusted Grey.

As for the cardinal, he had too many other problems to concern himself with how the crown was guarded. The archdiocese had a $2,000,000 deficit just for its schools, and Killane would be busy trying to raise it from the Rockefellers and the Tishmans. Reggel had done his reading.

While Isadore went off to find an usher, the captain completed his inspection of the gallery. There were four galleries in all. The two flanking the sanctuary were about fifty feet long and five feet wide, with three bays facing the high altar and its canopy. Two air blowers sat close to the bays and against the wall were winches for the chandeliers that hung from in front of the clerestory windows down to the sanctuary. It was here the Americans had posted their men during the Kennedy services, here and at the other galleries. Reggel approved.

He could be wrong; there might be no danger. Every day he read European papers for news of Odrich. Knowing how Odrich liked to live in style, he'd examined the guest list of every luxury hotel since the crown's return was announced. The only advantage he could be sure of was that he would know the church and Odrich wouldn't. There were only two sources for copies of the cathedral plans, the city and Columbia University, and for the next ten days they were the exclusive property of the Hungarian mission.

And if something did happen, that was why he had Grey.

Confident of that much, Reggel left the gallery by a winding staircase to find the wandering Jew.

Roman pursued survival on Staten Island. From the ferry slip he took a taxi through anachronistic small towns and woods on a road called Victory Boulevard.

He got out in the center of the island in a neighborhood made up of small factories and empty lots edged with linden trees. In the corner of a lot close by a park was a hunched aluminum trailer of the style popular twenty years before.

Roman entered without knocking, because only police or strangers knocked. Pulika Wells sat at a table. Except for a hat and a bright red kerchief around his neck he was naked to the waist, and his skin folded like worn leather over his stomach. A boy sat in a corner of the trailer mending a bellows.

"*Sarishan.*"

"*Sarishan,* Romano," Pulika said. "Sit down. I've been wondering when you would come around." He turned to the boy. "Tea for the Rom."

The boy put a kettle onto a hot plate and stood by it. Roman guessed he was no more than seven years old. He had black hair and blue eyes, a trait of the Wells clan left by their namesake, a bastard son of Charles II.

"My great-grandson," Pulika told Roman.

"He's handsome."

"He is an artist. It won't be easy for him being handsome and an artist. I'll keep him outside the city as long as I can."

Roman knew that Pulika's sons wanted their father to move into the city with them. His wife was dead and the boy's parents had been killed in an accident on the road. As it was, the boy went into the city only when Staten Island schools tried to find him and then just for the day. Like some of the old Rom, Pulika never passed a night inside a house voluntarily, and the boy lived with Pulika.

The *chal* served glasses of tea on an intricately etched copper tray.

"He made this," the old man told Roman with more pride than he hoped showed. "He will be better when his hands are stronger. If we had a horse he could ride, his hands would be stronger. It would have to be a gentle horse, but how many Rom here know horses?"

"Maybe he will get óne." The boy's blue eyes burned with excitement. Roman toasted him. "*Aukko tu gry, prala.* To your horse, brother."

After a rite of elliptical conversation, Roman laid his empty glass sideways, signifying that he wanted no more tea.

"You mentioned something about the Magyars to me once, uncle. I have some questions."

"I know. Come with me and you can ask while I work."

In back of the trailer was a shelter made of corrugated iron, its roof curved on the order of the "bender" wagons used by American Rom before they had cars. A tall, bony dog ran out of it and circled Pulika joyously. It was a "long dog," a breed of greyhound mongrel that could only be found in a Gypsy camp.

"Don't let the American Kennel Club get hold of you," Roman told the dog as he scratched its head.

Pulika's small, portable anvil was already set up under the shelter, its sharp base driven into the ground. The boy tended the forge, which was no more than a hole in the ground. He fed charcoal into the embers and fanned them with his mended bellows, a goatskin turned inside out with a slit for the air to enter and a pipe through one of the legs to allow a jet of air to exit. When the fire was going well, Pulika and Roman lowered a copper vat into the hole. In a matter of minutes the vat began turning to a deep purple. Pulika pulled an iron tube from a work chest, his old muscles standing like cords under his dark skin. He dropped it beside the vat and drew an *S* shape in the dirt with his finger.

"For a brewery. They can wait a month for a factory to do it or they can come to the Kalderash." He shrugged. "It's not the sort of fine work I used to do, but they will pay. I don't have any woman to tell fortunes for me anymore."

The boy sat cross-legged by the fire. Now that it was going well, he could work the bellows with his feet and play with the dog at the same time. The two men squatted down, and Roman shared his cigarettes.

"I heard you were involved with a piece of *sonakey* Magyar." Pulika squinted through the smoke.

"*The* piece of Magyar gold. Saint Stephen's Crown. I need to know what you know."

"Why not, Romano? Maybe the boy can learn something, too."

Pulika's voice lost his huskiness as it slipped into the rhythm of the storyteller. The dog lay down under the boy's hand. The vat changed from purple to red.

Pulika said he was a *sonakeyengro*, a goldsmith, when the war began. He was a young man, no more than forty, with his own camp. Things were not so bad at first because the Magyars were on the Germans' side and he could travel as long as he had what the authorities called an *Ausweis*, a special permit from a *Kommandant*, which was a German *guero*.

"But you pollute a stream and even the fastest fish die. Sometime around the fifth year of the war we were stopped by *gueri* in black uniforms. They said we were no longer considered Aryans, whatever that meant. Whatever we were if we weren't Aryans, it was a crime. So we were caught and taken to a camp ringed with barbed wire at Hopfgarten, which is near Salzburg in Austria. It was especially for Rom, a *Zigeunersammelplatze*, a Gypsy camping ground, they called it. You see, for a time they had killed us along with the Jews, but the Jews complained. They faced death with wails. We sang. After all, death is unavoidable. Fearing it wastes time. So, people face death in different ways and who can say which way is better? But how typical it was of our killers to respect this one complaint and no others. I could use another cigarette."

Roman lit one and gave it to Pulika.

"One morning, we found the gates open. All the guards had run away during the night and we heard that the Americans were coming. At once, everybody was in a bustle leaving the camp. We found a wagon and pulled it ourselves while the women rode, traveling over fields and avoiding the roads. We had not gone very far by the second day when we found the Magyars. There were six of them, all officers, and their car was on its side. They pointed guns at us but, believe me, they were more frightened than we were because the country was overrun with Americans and all the Germans were giving themselves up.

"They ordered us to help them get their car back on its feet. Once we did that, naturally they became friendlier and asked where we were going.

" 'Away from the dead swallow,' I told them.

"They laughed and said it was typical Gypsy nonsense, but it wasn't. I was bitter about all the good Rom dead.

" 'What did you do before the war?' they asked me.

"I was arrogant. I'm not so arrogant now that all I have to work with is iron pipes, but then I was."

The vat reached its hottest pitch, becoming a dull, shimmering green. The old man looked at the boy.

" 'I was a goldsmith,' I said. That was when they brought out their guns again and took me to the Holy Crown."

Six men sat in a room at the Commodore and took notes at a slide lecture.

The first slide showed the side door Killane used to enter the church from his residence. The ones following were close-ups of the lock and hinges.

"There's no alarm."

"No. Nor on any of the other doors," Odrich commented. "The cardinal is very set on this being a house of God. The locks are very simple, as you can see, because there are always ushers and maintenance men on duty."

He pressed a button and the projector's carousel moved a notch.

A slide of the side door leading to the administrative building appeared. It was in most ways identical with the first series.

"Instead of the cardinal's private sacristy, a room for the ushers is here. No doubt, the Hungarians will take it over."

Next came a slide of the rusticated wall surrounding the plateau from which the cathedral rose. Set into the wall was a door.

"From the foundation plans, this leads to the boiler room. You can see it is iron." A succeeding slide was of the outside lock. "A regular bolt mechanism from the shape of the impression. No bar."

"Then it would take us only a few minutes to get in. The police standing at the church won't be able to see that door."

"Fine, but you forget that Fifth Avenue has Cartier and Tiffany. There are patrols all the time. When we enter someone will let us in or we will have a key. There is one other way in."

A shot of the windows directly over the altar of the Lady Chapel appeared. A second slide of one of the chapel's side windows and a third on the outer of the side window's three lancets followed.

"The bottom panel opens for ventilation. Here Reggel has persuaded the cardinal to lay an electric strip between the panel and one above it."

"So, we cut through the glass, tape some copper wires to the contacts and then open the window, right?"

"There's still the problem of the glass. Not as much as in old stained windows with metal oxides all through the glass, but even having pigments burned into the surface means a difficult cut."

A discussion of techniques followed. Tapes were unreliable on uneven surfaces, suction cups were for movies. If metallic pigment permeated the glass, even a diamond saw could make too much noise. Would the light outside cast a shadow through the window? Madison Avenue was not the unlit thoroughfare most European churches were on. As the conversation became more intense it was carried on less and less in English and more in Italian. When he heard the same arguments twice, Odrich suggested it was time to stop for something to eat.

A buffet of melons and ham waited on the coffee table, and they relaxed while they ate by watching the eleven o'clock news. Midway into the news show the screen was filled with a drawing of the Holy Crown. From that, the broadcaster cut to a film of St. Patrick's and a subterranean hall, its walls lined with tables bearing vestments.

"It will be in the sacristy," one of the viewers announced.

The hotel room had been rented by Odrich's assistants with a credit card in the name of the Italian magazine *Oggi*. Odrich had found that clerks were less likely to remember faces when presented with an institutional identity. If the *Oggi* cards were stolen, that was in character. The card bearers had lost their own identities long before.

At the end of the war, children from Hungary, Czecho-slovakia, Yugoslavia and Poland had flowed into Italy. Out-side Trieste, they lived in a refugee camp called Padriciano, and there Odrich had gone looking for the brightest, strongest and least wanted of a displaced population. He offered money, education and names, and that was more than enough.

That was what Frederick Morton wanted and that was why he was in the room. Harlem was New York's Padri-ciano.

At first when the men approached him, Morton was suspicious. It was odd enough for whites to hang out around a Harlem swimming pool asking questions. But Harlem was a heroin land, a fantasy land. The mythical finger had pointed to him. If it was a white finger, it didn't matter. The black boy's sullenness dissolved into a practical assessment of a future that was impossible before. And Odrich made it easy. Morton didn't even have to return to his half a room on 120th Street. He checked into a hotel room Odrich reserved for him, he wore the clothes Odrich brought him. He didn't worry about labels being cut out; he wanted to cut out a whole past. The proof that he could do it were the men around him.

A film projector was set and loaded. Frederick Morton felt the beer pressing on his bladder and asked permission to use the bathroom.

"You don't have to ask," Odrich said. "You're one of us now."

The bathroom was hung with damp negatives. Prints floated in the tub. When he'd relieved himself, Morton took a closer look at them. They were nothing like the slides that had been shown in the other room, no doors or windows, locks or alarms. These were of priests and altars and communion rails.

The boy's curiosity was aroused. He opened the linen closet. On the shelves were the Minox cameras he'd been shown how to use. In the bottom of the closet was a square leather case that Odrich had brought that afernoon. If the boy's guess was right, the box held a silver goblet.

The case had a combination lock. Morton touched the lid and almost jumped when it moved. He lifted it again with both hands. With the top gaping open, he stood up and stared.

As Odrich guessed, he was a bright boy. Morton knew he was looking at the same crown he had seen on television minutes before.

CHAPTER
9

THE CAVALCADE TURNED up a cleared Fiftieth Street and drove along the south side of St. Patrick's, the cars' sirens giving the cue to the newsmen and photographers on the steps. At the barricades, Freedom Fighters who had been patient and silent began waving their signs and shouting. Isadore gave up making sense out of his walkie-talkie and handed it over with disgust. On the other hand, he couldn't translate what the protestors were yelling, and he had that to be thankful for.

As soon as the cars halted in front of the church, the mayor and his bodyguard emerged. The bodyguard ran up to the top of the stairs while the mayor helped the cardinal. Ambassador Nagy, the chief of the Hungarian mission, stretched his short legs in the company of the cultural representatives. With no clear plan, the diplomats, officials and squads of police formed two lines. Only then, Reggel opened a limousine in the middle of the line and directed his men out. They backed out, holding onto two brass-handled poles, two more men followed, holding the other ends of the poles, and in the middle was the metal coffer.

Roman waited inside the church in the organ loft with

Reggel's second-in-command, a Lieutenant Csonka. In the galleries, the rest of Reggel's squad stepped back into the shadows. The vestibule filled with staged tension, and as the doors opened the back pews lit up in the white glare of camera lights. The four men with the coffer entered, and the entourage followed. When enough dignitaries were inside they fanned out so that more pictures could be taken of the chest, which appeared progressively smaller in the flash of the strobes.

The procession moved down the aisle to the communion rail. There Killane said a few words, followed by a Hungarian cleric. This ceremony attended to, most of the dignitaries were departing. A small group followed the coffer around the ambulatory to the rear of the sanctuary, where they entered and descended the sacristy steps behind the high altar.

As he was instructed, Roman waited until Isadore had entered the church before he left the loft.

The coffer sat on a table covered with red velvet. Once Isadore brought Roman through the sacristy gate it was rolled closed and barred. Beyond a nervous glance, no one paid attention to the two men's entrance. Reggel hovered over the ancient chest.

Angels supported the Hungarian coat of arms on the chest's front. On top, three padlocks locked the lid's bar. Over the lips of the lid was a wax seal imprinted DEPARTMENT OF THE ARMY—ARCHIVES DIVISION.

Dr. Gyulos Andos, a small man in formal afternoon attire, held a blackened key.

"Dr. Andos was the last Hungarian scholar to see the crown before the war," Ambassador Nagy announced. "He will open the first lock."

Fumbling betrayed the doctor's eagerness. Finally, he had the key in the lock and it sprung open. The second key was given to a man called Szemely. He thrust it into his lock energetically.

"Not too hard, please," the doctor warned in Hungarian.

The lock opened and Reggel picked it up with the first. The last key was offered to Killane and the mayor, but they both demurred.

"If you insist," the Hungarian ambassador said. Pleased and sleek as a beetle, he inserted the key and twisted it.

Reggel took the final lock off the chest and swung the loose bars out of the way. With his first pull the wax seal broke. His second lifted the lid back to reveal the Hungarian state treasure in three velvet-lined compartments.

The royal scepter lay on the right. In a square compartment on the left was the Holy Apple, a gold orb with a cross. In the deep middle compartment on a velvet cushion was the Crown of Saint Stephen.

"It's different," the mayor blurted out. No offense was taken because it was what everyone was thinking.

"There is nothing like it," Andos answered with pride. "It is referred to in Vatican records as the *sanctissima corona*, the most holy crown. If it looks strange to you it is because it is like its people, half Western and half Eastern. Could you lift it, please, captain?"

Reggel brought the crown and its cushion out of the chest.

It was slightly larger than a human head. The lower diadem was green gold and the upper hemisphere red gold. On top was a small bulbous cross bent to the right. Attached to the diadem and lying in a curl on the cushion were fine gold chains.

"This was the gift of Pope Sylvester II to King Stephen, the first Christian King of Hungary." Andos pointed to the rows of red gold. "The Hungarian nation began by his coronation with this crown almost one thousand years ago. Each band is decorated with enamel plaques framed by filigree mountings set with gems and pearls. The bands are cracked from great age and as a result of being buried in many hiding places during the occupation of Hungary for hundreds of years by the Turks.

"The lower diadem was added, we believe, seventy years later. It was a gift of the Byzantine Emperor Michael Ducas to our King Géza for Hungary's help in time of war. It, too, is decorated with enamel plaques representing apostles and kings. The stones are contemporary except for the large faceted sapphire at the back, which was a seventeenth-century replacement. Above and below the headband are rows of pearls on a gold wire, and also around the top of the headband are translucent blue-green enamels with fish scale designs in alternating arch and gable forms decreasing in size from the front. There are none of these on the back half of the diadem, but there are pearls mounted on gold pins.

"The nine gold chains ending in semiprecious stones complete the diadem's 'stemma' form. It is the most perfect example of the Greek 'stemma' form left in the world today. And so you see what I mean. For Hungary, the crossroads of East and West, a symbol composed of two gifts from Rome and Constantinople. And now it goes home."

A photographer from the Communist Party paper *Nepsyabadsog* stepped forward and snapped a shot, the explosion of his bulb seemingly reflected a moment longer in the gold and gems than anywhere else in the room, but when everyone's eyes recovered, Reggel had replaced the crown in the chest.

After a final blessing by Killane, the chest was shut and padlocked. The sacristy gate was then unlocked for the dignitaries to leave for a reception at the Hungarian mission on Seventy-fifth Street. As their voices faded, Roman was amazed. The mayor was already talking about a skiing vacation in Chile.

Andos had recovered enough from his emotion to realize that the Gypsy was his counterpart.

"Does the mission know about this?" he asked Reggel.

"Mr. Grey's credentials have been checked most carefully."

Andos backed down under the force of Reggel's glower.

Csonka appeared at the sacristy gate to tell the captain the church was clear. Reggel and Roman fitted the carrying poles into slots on the coffer's sides. The two men lifted it off the table and carried it through the gate and up the sacristy steps. In the bay behind the altar another flight of stairs led directly under the sanctuary floor. It was guarded by a pair of double bronze doors inscribed REQUIESCENT IN PACE. Reggel unlocked them and swung open the way to the cardinal's crypt.

They carried the chest down into a short marble hall lit by inset fluorescent fixtures. At the end of the hall, directly under the high altar, was a vault seven feet deep and eleven feet wide. The longer wall was divided into fifteen marble panels in three rows. All the panels of the top row bore names etched in gilt of the men lying behind them. There were also prayers in Latin and English, and four of the panels displayed representations of a cardinal's wide-brimmed, flamboyantly tassled hat.

Isadore followed them into the crypt with the velvet-covered table, and they set the chest down on it.

Reggel looked around with satisfaction.

"The sacristy would never have done. Windows. Priests coming in and out. A fire. Anything could happen. But here? No one but—" He cocked his head to the wall of panels. "No way in but the stairs and an air hole. The altar above and stone below. The perfect safe."

"Yeah, this should really cement my popularity," Isadore said. "Excuse me."

The claustrophobia of standing in a stone grave drove him up the stairs. Once in the bay he breathed the fresh air gratefully, unconsciously searching the faraway ceiling, making out a star of ribs around a dove of peace. A warm nausea replaced his chill when he saw that under the dove was a bright drop of blood.

"The late cardinal's hat," Killane said conversationally by Isadore's side, making the policeman jump. The detective had not seen him return. Isadore looked back at the suspended dot of red.

"You must have seen a picture of it on his vault," the cardinal went on. "Nobody notices them because they're so far up, but all the cardinals' hats are up there. His is the only one that's still red."

He read the question in Isadore's mind.

"I don't know what they'll do about me. The synod of Vatican II decided they were a bit too extravagant with the tassels and all, so we don't wear them anymore. The young priests don't even wear a collar. So we substitute old disguises for new ones."

The other two men came out of the crypt. Roman was not surprised to see Killane. The cardinal had seethed throughout the ceremony in the sacristy. Reggel casually locked the bronze doors.

"Come with me, please," Killane ordered them. He

crossed himself, the only one to do so, and led them through the ambulatory to a side door between a chapel and a Pietà of Christ.

He shut the door behind them.

"This is my private sacristy. I know you've been eager to see it, captain. A photo of His Holiness, of myself and my family the day I was ordained, a crucifix of Our Lord, the hymn of Saint Patrick before Tara. A few chairs, a table, a wardrobe closet."

The cold eyes swept over the three men and rested on Reggel.

"Now I want you to show me something, my friend. In return for granting use of the crypt to keep the crown, you agreed that there would be no firearms on the church floor. You are wearing one right now."

The Hungarian was surprised but not ashamed. He spread his hands.

"I was wearing it at the airport. I simply forgot to remove it, Your Eminence."

It was the first time Roman heard Reggel use the title. It sounded sibilant on his lips.

"Your men in the sacristy, they also forgot?"

"How did you know that?"

They were interrupted by a knock at the door. Through it Monsignor Burns inquired whether Killane was ready to leave for the reception.

"In a minute, monsignor. Tell the organist he can go to the loft now and have the ushers open the doors."

He returned his attention to the men in the room.

"You know, captain, I had some doubts when I was created cardinal. The truth is that men like the monsignor are right. I do lack a certain sympathy; my faith could be less intellectual and more instinctive. But I see now some purpose in taking a cynical assistant of state and making a cardinal of him.

"Because I've been in Hungary and seen other secret police captains work, sitting in the last aisle and taking down the names of the worshipers or crossing priests off their 'approved' list. I know who you are and what you do and I won't allow the stench of it in this church. If I see one more jacket bulging with a gun on the church floor, the crown will leave the crypt and you can take your chances."

The Hungarian didn't flinch, just weighed his options.

"Very well, we will follow your orders."

Killane went to the door.

"God bless you," he said as an afterthought and left.

Reggel felt the holster under his arm ruefully, then returned to the ambulatory. A hand on his arm stopped him. Roman had followed him.

"There's something else," Roman said. "Your Dr. Andos gave a very good lecture."

"So?"

"I thought he couldn't speak English. That was one of the reasons I was chosen."

"Not you." Reggel's anger leaped to the surface. "Don't you give me trouble, Gypsy. I've had enough from that hypocrite in the cassock. I expect it from him but not from you."

"What do you expect from me?"

"If anything happens, don't blame me. Blame the priests and traitors who brought the crown here." The Hungarian's face was no longer the impassive mask he'd worn so far. He gestured at the sanctuary and the crypt beneath. "I only protect the crown. I did not arrange for this gruesome show."

Organ music swelled the air as the doors were opened to the public.

"We have a poet called Juhasz, Gypsy, whose friend was buried against his wishes in a church like this. Juhasz wrote, 'Here you lie in this paltry proletarian grave, in this capitalist filth of stone, bronze and granite, this abomination, this raving money-paradise, among dim fathers in marble strung around with white marble roses, their bronze hats and mustaches inclining to the shit that rains down from pigeons.'

"Here our crown lies in their crypt because there is no place safe in this cardinal's cathedral and it is surrounded by the expediency of enemies and the selfishness of renegades. Only I stand by the Holy Crown and I will do it any way I can."

He broke off and strode through the growing flow of tourists and worshipers. Roman stood where he was for a few more seconds and then took his time about reaching the vestibule where Isadore waited by a door.

"What was that all about?" the detective asked.

"Just finding out where we stood."

A pair of old women jostled Roman aside as they made their way in.

"Where do we stand?"

"We, as an old Hungarian expression puts it, are the fall guys."

CHAPTER
10

A SUMMER RAINSTORM had passed over the city during the evening services, and at the police sawhorses only a solitary man in a raincoat carried a sign that read FREEDOM FOR HUNGARY.

Reggel and Isadore laid wires to the photoelectric cells taped against the front of the choir stalls.

"You shouldn't listen to what that Gypsy has to say. When you know them longer you'll know better than to expect the truth, no?"

"There are worse things," Isadore told him.

"He is what he is."

Isadore pushed the three-pronged coupler into the control panel behind the altar.

Eight dull lights glowed around the sanctuary. Csonka stepped between two of them and a horn blared through the loudspeakers over the pulpit. Isadore pulled the socket out.

"The people will file along the ambulatory," Reggel said. "It is unlikely someone would not be seen by us, but in case there is a staged distraction this will warn us anyway."

The other cells were tested. Only two had to be re-adjusted.

"What do you mean by 'he is what he is'?"

Reggel rolled the cord up while Csonka taped the cells more securely.

"I know you are some sort of expert, sergeant, but how well do you really know Gypsies?"

"How well can anyone know them?"

"We know them," Reggel said significantly. "Items that a cardinal would not like said in his church."

Csonka pointed up to the gallery on the north side of the nave. Two poles held an American flag and another with the miter and keys to the Vatican. A third with the colors of Hungary was being hoisted into place next to them by Reggel's men. Isadore appreciated the fact that all the flags were outshone by the rose window, its colored glass burning like glowworms from the floodlights outside.

"Are you a squeamish man, sergeant?"

"Not very."

"Well, we'll see. Have you ever heard of the Siebenge-birge?"

Isadore bristled. "It's a mountain range in Germany."

"No. This one is a mountain range between the People's Republic of Hungary and the People's Republic of Ruma-nia. I think most people here know it better as Transyl-vania. The Siebengebirge is home for a tribe of Gypsies called the Netotsi. Tell me, what is your opinion of can-nibalism and people who practice it? This is an interesting custom, don't you agree?"

A bright spotlight was turned onto the bay from the gallery.

"Perhaps there was a reason."

"You give me a reason why they prefer carrion instead of freshly killed food. Did you know that in Hungary we have to pour carbolic acid on the carcasses we throw into the carrion pits so that the Gypsies won't dig them up? Or why when the Gypsy goes to the trouble of buying a chicken instead of stealing it, he asks the farmer to let it rot in the sun for three days?"

Isadore felt a prickly buzz on his spine. The words were too familiar to those he'd heard about another group.

"Pay no attention to him. A Gypsy is born with a lie in his mouth. This one is no different. Anyway, we're finished here," Reggel concluded. "Now we celebrate."

Isadore left first. His departure was noted by the lone picket across Fifth Avenue. A gray microbus with diplomatic plates arrived outside a transept door. A squad of Hungarian secret police entered the church, and shortly afterwards Reggel and four other men came out. Because of the church's illumination, Odrich saw him clearly.

Reggel was a little taller and much heavier, filled out from the lanky athlete Odrich remembered. The hair was the same wheat gold, in contrast to an almost Asian face. There was brusque command and physical strength instead of adolescent bravado, but the adolescent Odrich recalled was from a war thirty years old. No doubt the Hungarians had chosen the right man.

The microbus doors slammed and it started out for Madison Avenue.

Five Hungarians inside, seventeen patrolmen and plainclothesmen outside and surveillance cars. Odrich already knew that Reggel had chosen to do without the night shift of ushers and maintenance men.

Odrich discarded his picket sign and raincoat in a service alley and walked up Fifth. He passed Killane returning from the Hungarian reception without noticing, because he was intent on the art gallery windows. To him they were a chronicle of the decline of art, starting with the substitution of tempera for oil, a technological breakthrough that freed the Impressionists and sentenced everyone else to a future of spray paint and plastic. It was no wonder New York was the new center of the art world; it had been said, he remembered, that the best example of form following function was the ashtray. And would families eating fried chicken from cardboard containers be able to drive by junkyards piled high with rusting Calders?

On Seventy-fifth Street he turned off Fifth and headed for the inverted ziggurat of the Whitney Museum on Madison Avenue. Midway up the block the Volkswagen bus was parked in front of the faintly decrepit town house Hungary rented for its mission. Sounds of celebration leaked from it.

Odrich stopped at the Whitney next to a parked Lincoln convertible. Karl was at the wheel with another of the men from the Commodore.

"If he walks across the street, run him down," Odrich said casually as he studied the architecture of the museum. "Then throw the paint at the mission. I don't really care how political this looks as long as Reggel is dead. You'll find that's the only kind of politics that's understood."

Second Avenue from Seventy-seventh Street to Eighty-eighth is Central Europe on a straight line, running from Czechoslovakian restaurants to German *Brauhäuser* and from goulash to potato pancakes. Roman and Dany stopped in between at a Hungarian restaurant that offered "Real Gypsy Violinists" with a sign of sequins and black velvet.

"I thought you hated these places," Dany commented as they went in.

"Just slumming."

An emaciated maître d' in a tuxedo as stiff as a shell led them to a front table, but Roman chose one in the rear. They followed a yellowing wall-length mural of Budapest and the Danube to their new seats. It, like the wood trim and the bar, was painted a malevolent green. Dany felt the stares of the other patrons as she sat down and accepted a menu.

"You don't understand Hungarian, too, do you?" Roman asked, aware of her reaction to the diners, for the most part men dressed seriously in dark suits with shirts buttoned at the neck without a tie.

"No, thank God. Now I know why we never come here. But he wanted us to sit up front. Why?"

"That's a long story. Our maître d' is hovering. Would you like something to drink?"

They ordered *apéritifs*.

"He reminds me of someone. What was Bela Lugosi?"

"Please, let's not be prejudiced in return. But, since you ask, Hungarian. What else?"

The maître d' returned with a bottle of wine instead of the *apéritifs*. He spoke to Roman in Hungarian and poured enough wine to cover the bottom of his glass. Roman tasted the wine and nodded. A man at a nearby table raised his glass and toasted the Gypsy. Dany felt the tension ease.

"What did I miss?" she asked when the maître d' left, a more human smile on his face.

"He asked if I wouldn't prefer a Hungarian wine more, and I said the one he brought us was as sweet and bountiful as the district he was born in. They speak with a twang in Badacsony. His friend appreciated that. In other words, I wormed my way into their good graces."

"I didn't hear anything."

"A Hungarian twang."

Dany tasted the wine herself. It was white and strong. She looked around again. Roman had brought about the desired effect; what had seemed sinister was now cozily foreign. The restaurant proprietor and the maître d' bowed from the bar.

"They're not so bad." She looked at her menu. "I'm starving."

"Now there's a progression of thought."

When Roman tried to order a dinner, the maître d' was dogmatic about his own suggestion. It sounded like a four-course meal to Dany, and when Roman accepted the maître d' left with an air of personal satisfaction.

"You're right, there is a twang," she said.

"And the more you drink, the stronger it gets."

A man with the shape and some of the coloring of an avocado came out through the kitchen doors. He wore little dagger mustaches under his nose, an embroidered felt vest, a red silk sash at his belly, and he carried a violin. After one look at Roman he vanished back in the kitchen and reappeared without his instrument.

"Romano, what are you doing here?" he demanded as soon as he slipped into a chair at their table. Up close, Dany saw the musician appeared less ridiculous and his eyes were darting and intelligent. He was also uncomfortable. Roman called for another glass. "Romano, are you trying to make a fool of me, seeing me like this?"

"Tomo is a great musician," Roman told Dany in English. She understood; she wasn't supposed to know Romany at all in front of the indignant Gypsy. What mattered was Roman's confidence that she would.

Tomo Tomeshti forced his round face into a polite smile.
He'd heard about Roman's *gaji*. At the moment, though, he
was as furious as a man caught wearing a tutu.

"The problem with being a great musician like Tomo is
that he doesn't want friends hearing him play 'restaurant
music.' If Tomo played here the way he could, no one
would eat and he would lose his job. He wants you to understand this."

"The point is I look like an idiot in this outfit. Why are
you here?" Tomo repeated in Romany.

"About a horse," Roman answered in kind.

Tomo blinked and took a first sip of wine.

"Your brother is still at Belmont, isn't he?"

"Yes," Tomo said.

"I need a gentle horse with some years left in him.
Naturally, I thought of the Tomeshtis. Not everyone can
be trusted these days."

"True." Tomo's wrath subsided. A horse was an entirely
different matter. Tomo had to dress in Gypsy clothes and
play in restaurants in order to follow the races. Unfor-
tunately, his knowledge was better than his luck. He asked
for a cigarette. "I'm glad you explained this. Otherwise,
Romano—"

"Of course," Roman said meekly.

The tables close by carried on their conversations with
half an ear to the two Gypsies. Tomo's mahogany face
gleamed in the serene contemplation of horses.

"You understand that thoroughbreds are not cheap."

"No," Roman corrected, "a gentle horse. None of those
crazy thoroughbreds. Good-looking, gentle, something a
boy can ride and be proud of."

"A boy? Romano, when we were boys we raced stallions
bareback. What kind of boy?"

"A *chal* that never rode before."

Tomo grimaced. In New York it was possible. He strug-
gled to bring his imagination to a lower plane.

"I suppose it can be done. My brother is very good at
arranging these things. Still, it won't be cheap. Shipping the
horse, providing some feed, one thing and another."

"Certainly. I leave that all up to you. And when it's
going to arrive, let me know. Just so some scoundrel doesn't

try to ruin your good name by livening up a nag with a plug of ginger."

"Understood. And I will bring a banker to look at your money and a doctor to check your sex."

Dany caught enough to understand that they had negotiated with an eloquent bluntness. When they reached agreement, they drank on it.

The meal arrived. Rather than the four-course dinner Dany expected, it was one dish prepared especially by the chef: *ciganypecsenye hideg koritessel,* pork with cold vegetables, Gypsy-style. Tomo went off to the kitchen and reentered with his violin on a dramatic chord.

A gray microbus pulled up in front of a hydrant outside the restaurant. The driver got out and helped Dr. Andos emerge from the back, while more men got out on the street side. Reggel parked behind it alone in an old Chrysler limousine.

Between streetlights a block down, a third car parked.

The maître d' flourished a clean tablecloth and set a service for the new party. There were bottles on the table before the silver and the Hungarians toasted each other. Andos could barely keep his head up. Tomo tucked the violin under his chin and played louder. Reggel stomped his foot and kept time with the cigarette in his hand.

Roman and Dany were almost finished, and Roman called for the check. Instead, the maître d' bent over the Hungarian's table and pointed to the rear of the restaurant.

"Ciganyi!"

Reggel stood up. He waved for Roman to join the larger table. When Roman shook off the invitation, Reggel weaved his way through the tables toward them.

"If the Gypsy won't go to the Magyar, the Magyar will go to the Gypsy," he said as he took a chair and put down the bottle he'd brought.

Dany took her cue from Roman, who returned Reggel's smile. For a moment she thought Reggel was going to say something vulgar about her being with Roman. Suddenly, he filled their glasses from his bottle.

"This is Tokay Eszencia. Five hundred dollars a bottle. Wine that is so sweet and ripe it doesn't need to be pressed, it runs from the grape. As beauty and grace flow from you," he told Dany sincerely. "I knew our expert had the best of taste."

Reggel's high cheeks were flushed with drinking and his movements had an awkward formality. The Eszencia was very sweet. Dany was shocked; she could tell from Roman's glance that Reggel hadn't lied about the cost. The Hungarian filled her glass again, generously.

"Very good," she said.

"You'll get used to it," he promised.

"The reception is over?" Roman asked.

"Ended. All the weaklings have passed out, so we came here to carry on. This is not a night when a Hungarian should be asleep."

"Aren't you afraid to come here?" Dany wanted to know.

"Because we are Communists?" Reggel grinned. "We are Hungarians. No true Hungarian can hold it against us for retrieving the Holy Crown. Besides, what would be more perfect than to spend this glorious evening in the company of my Gypsy and his lovely lady? This is no night to hold grudges."

Reggel possessed an animal energy that was near Gypsy. He described how Eszencia regularly revived kings on the brink of death. What intrigued Dany more was his intimacy with Roman. All his efforts were designed to seduce Roman's friendship more than hers. Even his insults had a fierce amiability. When one of his friends asked Reggel to return to the front of the restaurant, the captain sent him back with a sharp word.

"You see, the Gypsy and I go back a long, long time," he told Dany, his eyebrows raised.

Tomo's eyes were closed, but he moved through the tables without brushing a chair. Already, he had abandoned the usual restaurant repertoire, and the patrons were listening with their forks and knives untouched beside their plates. His bow drew slowly over the bass string.

"I never heard of the Netotsi before," Dany said.

Reggel loomed over the table to tell her, his eye on Roman. "A shame. But, perhaps, they should best be forgotten."

"She might be interested," Roman said. "I think keeping

Gypsies as slaves for three hundred years is interesting. The slaves who escaped were called Netotsi. The army recaptured some and tortured them until they confessed anything they were asked. That way the Hungarian bishops could approve a general slaughter of cannibals instead of families running for their lives."

The presence of another Gypsy awakened Tomo. Thoroughbreds minced through his mind. God said that Gypsies could eat anything but the flesh of a horse. There was no wealth but gold and horses. From his six-stringed violin, he drew the lament of the *Khassiyem:* "I am lost, father, brother. My favorite horse has run away. Yes, last night I couldn't sleep. I loved her."

"Yet you are different from the other *ciganyi*. A Gypsy who deals in art, who impresses cardinals and lovely women. You impress me. Do you know when I compliment you?"

"There was a queen once who wore the Crown of Saint Stephen," Roman said. "She loved Gypsies, too. To show her love she tried to make them into Hungarians.

"She had their horses and wagons taken away so they couldn't wander and she outlawed Romany so they couldn't conspire without being understood. As her greatest act, she had all their children taken away so that they could be free of their parents' influence. A great caravan formed of children and babies. The Gypsies clung to the wheels of the carts and killed themselves while they could still see their children and their children could still see them.

"The plan of this virtuous queen failed. The children turned into Gypsies and it was decided that the reason was they were born criminals and no one could help them. Of course, she was a saint to try."

Tomo plucked his violin like a guitar. The restaurant's owner stood transfixed as his Gypsy sang in a way he'd never heard before. "Cut from Heaven's tree I have two leaves, see! One says, 'You are poor.' One says, 'You are free.' "

"There is a saying in Hungary," Reggel told Dany as he filled her glass again. " 'Give a Magyar a glass of water and a Gypsy and he becomes drunk.'' We even have a word for it: *mulatni*. It means to enjoy oneself with a Gypsy. You must know what it means."

Tomo was ready. The men at the tables passed cigarettes back and forth in silence, a conspiracy of silence urging the Gypsy on.

The first part of a rhapsody is built on the Hungarian love of melancholy, of endless, repetitive tragedy. It is a *lassu*, a memory of things lost, the notes ending so abruptly that pauses become echoes. Tomo's slim voice turned rough with a bitterness that was improvised and real.

"The days are shorter, the nights longer. Why do I shiver? Why do they say the Gypsies have changed? I don't understand."

The song, a variation in monotone, stirred restlessly as if it were in pain, repeating itself a fifth higher.

"Watch," Reggel whispered to Dany.

Again and again the cry came. Explosively, Roman's hands came down on the table and he yelled out to Tomo. The bow leaped and ripped over the violin in instantaneous transformation, freed of regret. Now Tomo was the Gypsy violinist Reményi who played the Hungarian armies into battle in the wars of liberation. Reggel and the others joined in the *friss*, singing and slapping the tables, wine bottles ringing in 4/8 time, the men's faces flushed with emotion. Tomo neared Roman's table. Reggel's voice boomed out words Dany couldn't understand. Roman sang them, too, but on his face and Tomo's was a subtle difference, a wild strain of mockery that sweetened their voices and made the song all the more unreal.

Then the third part of the rhapsody, the *czardas*, began. Dany found it hard to believe there was energy left to be tapped, but the war song was faint in comparison to the erupting orgy of the *czardas*. This was the final, total expenditure of sensation, the hymn of the Magyar raiders whipped into a frenzy by Gypsy slaves. The song was as illogical. There was no beginning or end to it, nor any line of development; it lasted as long as Tomo's bow could move and there was a voice left to match it.

In the end there was only Roman and Reggel and then Roman alone, and the words veered sharply from

Hungarian to Romany so that she understood the last stanza of an old Lovari song:

"When a dead swallow flies, and follows us over the river, Oh, we'll forget the wrongs we've met. But till then, Oh never. Brother, of that be certain."

There was no clapping, just as there would be no applause for a death or lovemaking. The patrons, numbed, stuffed money into Tomo's vest and stumbled out of the restaurant. Tomo, ten pounds of sweat gone, collapsed in a chair. Dany realized with amazement that an hour had passed since the beginning of the rhapsody. Not one drink or dinner had been ordered during that period. Reggel's party stood at the door and waited for him to join them.

Roman alone took mercy on the proprietor and ordered a dinner.

"You already ate," the maître d' told him.

"This one is for the violin."

The men in the convertible watched as Reggel helped Andos into the microbus and scolded him the way a father might a naughty boy. He talked loudly to the bus driver but his words were lost in the sound of the traffic.

The microbus drove off, leaving Reggel alone under the restaurant canopy. The convertible began pulling out. A couple came out of the restaurant. The girl was typically American. The man was black, they thought at first, or Spanish.

"It's the antique dealer."

"Gypsy? With her?" The other man leaned forward.

"We'll wait until they move away."

Reggel didn't leave them. All three got into the old Chrysler.

"Your fortune?" Roman couldn't help being amused. "You want your fortune told?"

"What better night? I am full of *czardas*, of *mulatni*. Now is the time to have my fate read by a Gypsy."

"Not this Gypsy."

"No, no, never. I heard the way you ended the song. You're dangerous. I wouldn't ask you to tell my fortune."

"Who then?" Dany asked.

"Look around." Reggel waved his arm. "I have been in this city six years. In that time there are Gypsy women everywhere, a fortune-teller for every street." He put his finger to his eye. "Always a sign of an economic downturn, mark my words." He laughed and slapped Roman's back. "Am I right or not? If you want to know how a country's economy is doing, count its fortune-tellers."

He started the car and they swung out into the street.

"What do you want to know?" Roman asked.

"You're laughing at me, Gypsy."

"Yes, I am. That's one of my privileges, Magyar. But tell me what you're after."

Reggel tapped his chest.

"Tonight I am after the truth. Tonight I am on a search and a Gypsy will lead me."

"You've had too much wine. You're drunk."

"With Gypsies. You are my good luck, Romano Gry. Did you know that? You are the Holy Crown's good luck."

"You're wrong again. I don't want any part of the crown. When this week is over, I'll walk away and forget about the two of you."

"Fine, walk away then. Now, take me to my fortune."

CHAPTER
11

VERA PULNESHTI'S FORTUNE-TELLING *ofisa* was on Canal Street where it divided Chinatown and Little Italy. She came to the door wearing a dragon robe and eating a pizza.

"Romano, what are you doing here? It's two o'clock. I have four welfare offices to go to in the morning."

Her "tea room" was decorated with the appropriate symbols of yin and yang and Sicilian Evil Eye charms. In a back room, Dany could see children watching a color television. They also seemed to be listening to a radio and a record player.

"It's very important that he gets his fortune told tonight," Roman said.

"I have to get these kids to bed sometime, Romano. Your friend is getting married in the morning or what? Why is he in such a hurry?"

"Aren't you supposed to be able to tell me that?" Reggel asked.

Vera fixed him with a black glare. She set the slice of pizza down and wiped her mouth and hands, then she pulled a pin from her bun of hair and let it cascade down her back. The Chinese robe turned from housecoat to royal gown.

She slapped up the front of a rolltop desk. The pigeon-holes inside were stuffed with tools of her trade.

"Tarot, Gypsy Tarot, I Ching, throwing sticks, palm, sun chart, tea leaves. Name it."

"I brought my own cards," Reggel said.

Vera nodded with the hauteur of a queen accused of spitting in a public place. Expertly, she separated the aces and face cards from Reggel's deck and gave the rest back. She shuffled the cards she kept standing up without once taking her eyes from his.

"Take four and put them in a row on the table."

Reggel did as she told him.

"Turn over the one on the far left."

It was the ace of spades, upside down.

"A violent end," Vera intoned. More casually, she added, "You can forget about the other cards."

Reggel shook his head with disappointment.

"I hoped for a little more, you understand. How much do I owe you for this?"

Vera looked down her hooked nose at him. The nostrils flared.

"Nothing," she dismissed him.

Reggel shrugged and put his wallet away. Roman and Dany waited by the door. Vera picked up her pizza.

"On the other hand," she began in an offhand way.

". . . there is a charm I can buy," Reggel finished for her in Romany.

Vera scowled and her eyes jumped from Reggel to Roman.

"Who is this man? Romano, I want to talk to you."

"Not now, Vera."

She advanced on the door, waving her slice of pizza.

"You want some cards read? I'll show you some cards read."

Roman pulled Dany and Reggel out. When they reached the bottom of the stairs they looked back up. Peering down over the railing with Vera were five children of varying ages, all hurling curses and one or two throwing food.

"I think she liked you," Roman told Reggel when the three of them had escaped outside.

There were even fewer cars on Canal Street then and most of them headed for the Manhattan Bridge. One or two neon lights on the Chinese side of the traffic were still lit, pastel characters against the dark blue of the night.

"It is late," Reggel said reluctantly.

The air was cool at this seam between hot days and he slapped his hands together.

"Come on," Roman said. "We can't miss early mass."

On the way home, Dany slept on Roman's shoulder while Reggel drove alone in front. Traffic was light and the Chrysler cruised at sixty. Roman was content to watch the occasional lights of barges in the river.

"She's asleep already," Reggel said.

Roman looked forward to the oval of Reggel's eyes in the mirror.

"Isn't it a shame?" he said. "If you'd known about her, you wouldn't have had to threaten the Rom in Hungary."

Reggel drove up the ramp to the East River Drive and said nothing. The window was open an inch and air blew at his hair, worn long in the Hungarian fashion rather than in any attempt at style. The flesh that age added to his face hadn't smoothed the massive cheekbones. If Vera shook his self-confidence it didn't show. Reggel might have been driving by the Danube.

"Don't underestimate me," he answered finally.

The Manhattan Bridge receded on the right and the Williamsburg Bridge approached two miles ahead. Cars surrounding the Chrysler moved to one side of the highway to exit. Reggel pushed his foot down on the accelerator and picked up speed on the empty highway. The one other car with them, a convertible, did the same.

The convertible moved away from Reggel's rearview mirror to his side mirror and began sliding up to pass. He moved the Chrysler a foot over to give the other car more room. The Twenty-third Street exit was coming up, where the drive would curve right and head for the Midtown Tunnel. Reggel glanced over at the convertible as it pulled alongside. There were two men in it, and the one on the passenger side was staring back at Reggel.

The convertible inched forward so that its door was on a line with the Chrysler's bumper. Reggel waited until the car edged closer without passing. He reached for his gun.

"Get down!" he yelled to Roman and Dany.

The man in the passenger seat turned completely around, facing Reggel with what looked like a red plastic pillow. He shouted something at his driver and let go of the pillow, which didn't fly away in the wind the way a pillow should but rolled ponderously in the air, bloated and carmine, directly into the Chrysler's windshield. It exploded in rays of red paint, covering not only the windshield but the limousine's side windows, the wind spreading it to coat every inch of glass.

The Chrysler was in the middle lane when the bag hit. Two seconds elapsed before Reggel found the window handle, rolled it down completely and put his head and shoulder out. By then it was too late to overcome the car's momentum.

A bumper dug into the metal rib separating north- and southbound traffic and the limousine's rear end fanned out, driving it into the rail at a steeper angle. Cartwheels of sparks flew around Reggel's face as he fought to force the steering wheel to the right with one hand. The heavy car shuddered, nearing the roll point.

Just as the highway straightened, the steering wheel snapped out of Reggel's hands. The car swayed into the barrier with its side, sheets of sparks following the car. He regained control of the wheel and eased off the barrier. From his side window he could only see his own lane and the southbound traffic.

"They're a hundred feet ahead in the right lane."

Reggel glanced into the car at the sound of the Gypsy's voice. Roman had moved to the front seat and rolled down the right side window. In between them, the windshield rippled in tides from the wind. Red streaks matted Reggel's hair, and Roman thought for a moment the Hungarian was shot, then realized it was paint that had come in when the bag hit.

"Where are they now?" Reggel asked.

"Coming back."

Reggel seesawed the wheel to check whether the fender

wings were bent into the tires. They weren't. When he put
his head out as far as he could, he could see the convertible slipping closer. Delicately, he steered into the
middle lane. From the windshield back, the Chrysler was
entirely red.

The convertible's brake light lit up. Reggel fishtailed into two lanes to avoid it. When he returned to the middle
lane the convertible had vanished. Roman tapped him on
the shoulder.

"In back."

The rear window was striped with paint, but in his side
mirror Reggel made out the convertible's bumper just
behind him. The convertible rammed him at sixty, driving
the Chrysler toward the barrier. Reggel stepped on the
accelerator and steered away with one hand. The convertible hit again. The Chrysler's left headlight exploded
against the barrier before Reggel escaped back to the
middle of the highway.

The East River Drive is a relative straightaway up to
125th Street, and the two cars were a third of the way
there when they passed the Midtown Tunnel. Arc lights
shot past the blind windshield like phosphorus bullets.
Reggel took his hand off the wheel long enough to throw
his gun into Roman's lap. It was slightly smaller than
a .45, with the brand name WALTHER across the grip.

"I can't do both," Reggel said.

"Don't take it, Roman."

Reggel pulled his head in enough to give Dany a furious
stare in the rearview mirror.

"Don't be an idiot. He has to."

"He doesn't. You can just stop."

By way of explanation, Reggel's foot let up on the
accelerator. At once, the convertible smashed into the
back, forcing the limousine out of the middle lane to the
low, concrete guard curb along the outside. The collision
threw Dany to the floor. She tried rising but fell with each
heave of the cars.

"Will you do something now, Gypsy?"

Roman squeezed out the window, holding the gun in his
left hand. Dany's yells were lost in the grinding of chrome
on chrome. Wind wrapped hair around his eyes as the con-

vertible swung in and out of view. Reggel's automatic felt
unfamiliar and useless, but Roman climbed half onto the
roof despite the bucking, until he was sure there was no
way he could fire around the bulk of the limousine.

The Chrysler bounced off the guard curb once before
Reggel bullied the speedometer up to ninety and pulled
away from the convertible's grip. The straightaway was
approaching the steep curve of an overpass, and looming
beyond was the traffic of the Triborough Bridge. Reggel
had surprised himself by staying on the road as long as he
had; he wouldn't have a chance once they hit the overpass
and the cars. The convertible gave them a final shove and
he corrected the wheel. The Gypsy was back in the car.
Reggel blinked the water out of his eyes and said nothing.
His stiff hand tightened on the wheel as the car lights
around the curve became separate and distinct.

Roman fired. The bullet traveled twenty inches from the
front seat before smashing through the center of the
windshield, leaving a small hole but a wide honeycomb
pattern of shatterproof glass.

He fired through the left side of the windshield in front
of Reggel and put a third bullet through the right. Swinging the gun's butt end, he punched out the crystalized
glass, with each swing more of the windshield disinte-
grating and more of the highway appearing. At the end,
he was peeling a wall of safety glass over the dashboard
as the wind blew in long strands of red paint.

"Yes," Reggel shouted. He helped Roman pull the last
brilliant wall of glass inside the car. Sitting back, he
gripped the wheel with both hands.

Roman climbed into the rear with Dany. She covered
her ears.

He fired two bullets through the rear window, aiming
high so that they would pass over the car behind. When he
broke through the glass he saw the convertible falling back
fast, confused by the shots and presenting a low profile. A
mile behind them followed the siren and floating red and
yellow lights of a patrol car.

Aggressively, Reggel swerved the limousine into the
path of the convertible, but at the last possible moment the
other car took advantage of the bridge ramp and left the

highway. The Chrysler met the bridge's exiting traffic and coasted to the first emergency zone on the side of the road to wait for the police.

"*Ciganyi, ciganyi,*" Reggel said as he kissed Roman on the cheeks.

In the glare of the arc lamp coming through the empty windshield the three people inside the car seemed to be sitting on beds of pink diamonds.

CHAPTER 12

THE HOLY CROWN rested in the middle of the sanctuary. When it had been removed from its iron coffer it was merely beautiful. In the colored daylight pouring through the stained-glass windows, the crown came alive.

From the pews, looking at it against the altar's gilt canopy and the cobalt blue of the Lady Chapel windows, the crown's sea-color enamels shimmered, animating Byzantine saints around a ring of green gold. The procession in the ambulatory, viewing the crown against the soft russet of the older clerestory windows, saw primarily a Roman dome of red gold, the bows studded with the fire of garnets and amethysts, stones backed with gold foil to reflect the light. The stand was set into the top of the crown, allowing the gold chains to hang their full length and giving it a sense of levitation magnified by the angle of the small cross balancing on its top.

Reggel looked down from the gallery. A step behind him, Csonka held a rifle out of view. There was another rifleman in the opposite gallery and two more in the galleries over the nave. The men sitting on the aisles in the front pews were his, and photoelectric beams squared the

sanctuary. No one could join the procession without passing more of his squad and a metal detector with the coy
trademark "Friskem." Even so, Reggel's nerves lay close
to the surface.

The crowd swelled at lunchtime, until Isadore had to
send more men to the front of the church to control the
flow. Around 2:30, the mass of people had gone and
Isadore and Reggel retired to the administration building
to get something to eat.

A sergeant from BOSSI joined them. The fact that
BOSSI is not, for public consumption, supposed to exist
accounts for the different names it has gone by—Bureau
of Special Services and Investigation, Neutrality Squad,
Public Relations Squad and Special Investigation Sec-
tion—but policemen with affectionate directness just as
often call it the Red Squad.

"You're going to help me?" Reggel responded with an
acid smile.

"We carry out surveillance on all groups, left or right,"
the man from Bossi told him. "We're just as interested in
identifying the men in that car last night as you are. The
Central European desk might well have their pictures on
file if they were Freedom Fighters."

Reggel swabbed a slice of bacon fat on his bread and
noticed the large black display case the sergeant carried.
Isadore ate a pastrami sandwich with mustard.

"You think a captain of state security wouldn't know a
Freedom Fighter if he saw one?" Reggel commented.

"Captain, we run one hundred thousand security checks
a year. We manage to keep an eye on you, the American
Nazi Party and eighty thousand illegal aliens. I'm hardly
going to open our files for you, but you need our help.
This is the city you're dealing with now, not the security
arrangements for a small mission."

Rebuked, Reggel nodded.

"The red paint is a strong indicator this was a political
act," the sergeant pointed out.

"The color of the paint?"

"Yes."

"Sergeant, look up at the ceiling. Tell me, what color are
my eyes? If you can, I'll let you help me."

"Why, they're brown."

"No, no, sergeant. In Hungarian."

The sergeant looked down.

"You're not serious. You're not going to refuse my help for a stupid reason like that? So what if I don't speak Hungarian? I work on the Central European desk. That's nine different countries."

"That's eight too many. No, thank you, sergeant." Reggel wiped his fingers before shaking hands. At the door he said, "By the way, my eyes are *barna*."

Isadore wrapped the remains of his sandwich in a paper bag.

"You're loaded with charm, captain."

"Why should I be charming to a spy? Besides, the men in the car could have been anyone. Here, people kill people they've never met. A stranger comes into your home and kills you. He meets you on the highway and tries to run you off the road."

"If it's as simple as that, why are you demanding that the priests be searched before they leave the church?"

"I don't like priests."

As they crossed back to the church, they saw the first full-scale demonstration on Fifth Avenue. The protestors shouted "Freedom for Hungary" in English and Hungarian. For all Reggel's professed indifference, Isadore caught his eye roaming over the faces at the barricades. After a minute of listening, the two officers went back inside the cathedral.

With each passing hour the light from the windows shifted around the crown, throwing one gold bow in filigreed relief, sending another into an amber haze. Occasionally, it burst into flame from the flash of a camera smuggled into the congregation, and there would be a slight disturbance as Reggel's men located the photographer.

The crowd grew in size again after five, and the pews were full by evening mass. Ushers locked the transept doors. The red ropes that had directed the procession around the ambulatory were used to reserve the first three rows for special guests. The mayor had left on his vacation, but there were the governor, ambassadors, museum representatives and a Papal Nuncio. In the rear of the congregation, Dany sat with Roman.

A new procession appeared, a train of white led by acolytes casting plumes of incense. There were two cardinal's miters, Killane and the Primate of Budapest, and behind them in the dress of his order the Abbot of the Benedictines, evangelizers of the Magyars. Reggel switched off the photoelectric cells just as the procession passed through the communion rail and up the sanctuary steps.

From the loft under the rose window, an organist magnified Brahms and a rifleman watched for the smallest suspicious movement from below.

CHAPTER
13

ON THE SECOND day of the crown's display, a young black maintenance worker emerged from the boiler room exit in the wall along the Fifty-first Street sidewalk. He carried a mop and pail to the curb. A patrolman on the corner started toward him for a moment, then saw the green uniform and waved.

Morton bent between two cars and poured a stream of dirty water from the pail. Still leaning over, he flipped open the headlight cover of the car to his right. Instead of lights, the socket held a gray waterproof plastic bag. He dropped the bag in the pail and shut the cover.

Inside St. Patrick's, he refilled the pail with water and added enough soap to turn the water milky; then he carried his pail and mop to the sanctuary. Another maintenance man polished the bronze doors to the crypt while one of the Hungarian guards stood over him.

He approached them and asked for the keys to the sacristy. The older maintenance man had just finished mopping the sacristy floors, but he was Spanish and he didn't want to expose his bad English in front of the guard. He gave Morton the keys.

Morton rolled the sacristy gates open and went directly to the room on the right of the hall. It was the least used of the changing rooms, furnished only with chairs, a *prie-dieu* and a tall stand-up closet. He opened the closet door and placed the dripping bag inside.

On the way out, he asked the other maintenance man why he didn't say the sacristy was already done. The Hungarian ignored a conversation he didn't understand anyway and stared at the crown.

At the Commodore, Odrich washed skin bronzer off his fingers before he put on his ecclesiastical collar. He ducked his head forward to the mirror, snapping the collar's fake button at the back of his neck. The front of his skull was freshly shaven and artificially tanned.

In the other mirrors the other men changed into their black suits, black dickeys and collars.

On the way out they exchanged their guns for breviaries.

CZARDAS

CHAPTER
14

IT WAS STILL dark on the third day of the crown's exhibition when Isadore picked up Roman. The detective was red-eyed and irritable.

"Isn't it a little early for mass?"

"Forget about your Hungarians. This is a bit of the home town."

The sun rose on the East Side, making the tops of the apartment buildings a crisp necropolis against a yet clean sky. The East River Drive passed over shadows on stilts. Roman yawned and stretched as dawn spread over Queens.

They took the drive up the Harlem River, and the brighter the day became the dirtier it got. At 178th Street they crossed the Harlem to the Bronx. Signs pointed to the Major Deegan Expressway and Yankee Stadium, but Isadore turned off back to the river. He stopped on a pot-holed street serving rotting quays underneath the 100-foot arches of an unused bridge.

"Highbridge Aqueduct," Isadore said, "Private property of any junky willing to make the climb."

A homicide van and two unmarked police cars were on the sidewalk. Two black patrolmen and a black detective stood on the cement collar of an arch that stepped into the river. The detective waved a flashlight at Isadore.

"You're back," he said. The detective's attitude toward Roman was composed more of lack of sleep than curiosity.

"How are you doing?"

"It's a bummer. We thought it would be easier when day came? That water's as dark now as it ever was."

Children in grease-colored clothes watched from a pier of car chassis as Roman followed the detectives onto the pile's cement buttress. On the other side of the pile one black and one white detective looked down at the water. Isadore took a wad of gum from his mouth and threw it as far into the river as he could. By now, Roman understood that the sergeant was resuming a watch begun hours before.

"This was the greatest bridge in America when it was built," Isadore muttered.

The stone piers in the middle of the bridge had been replaced by one elongated steel arch. A rope hung down from it a short jump from the abutment. Between the detectives lay a forensic field kit and a green canvas bag.

New children gathered on the trash heap, and the policemen kept their watch, staring at scum turned a tawny, molten glow by the rising sun. Suddenly the gilt was broken by a surfacing diver in a scuba suit. He crawled up on the abutment dragging what he found by its hand. He spit out his mouthpiece.

"Roll out the bag."

It was the body of a black man. The film covering him made it impossible to tell how old he was, and when the detectives hauled on his jacket sleeve, discolored water spurted between their fingers.

"We found him," Isadore yelled up, and for the first time Roman was aware of police on the bridge walkway.

The face was cleaned enough for Roman to see it was a boy. The black detective swore.

"It's Morton, okay."

"We have the fingerprints then," Isadore said. "Give us a fast cause of death."

A pink froth from the nostrils indicated that the boy had

died of drowning. The black detective dictated the *in situ* report with regained professionalism.

"Laceration on the wrist and forehead." His finger probed through the boy's short Afro. "At least one laceration on the left temple." The jaw pulled open. "The tongue cut, possibly self-inflicted." There was a pause as he spread the boy's nostrils wide. "Damn, damn, damn. This foam, it may be junk."

He went to the boy's arm and examined the inside of the elbow.

"Shit, he went back. Overdose. Have the lab look for morphine in the bile."

The detective let the thin black arm drop. "Tell me this doesn't make sense."

Isadore kneeled beside the boy. The diver sat with his flippers dangling over the water, smoking a cigarette.

"Look at this." Isadore pulled the boy's head to the side, exposing the neck. There was a barely discernible puncture in it.

"A hot shot," the black detective said. "Some bastard surprised him with a hot shot of junk."

"Then they gave him the shot in the arm." Isadore nodded. He pushed himself up with both hands and stood beside Roman. "Oh, boy. Let's get out of here."

By climbing vandalized steps, Isadore and Roman were able to work their way to the top of the old bridge. Each end of the walkway was blocked by particularly ugly barricades of corrugated metal and barbed wire. Along the Harlem, the other bridges and highways were already filled with morning traffic.

"God, you can't get a breath of fresh air in this town." Isadore rubbed eyes that were bloodshot and dry. "Did you ever see that kid before, Roman?"

"Never."

"Name was Frederick Morton. He grew up on a dozen different streets but he was a Boy Scout. Merit badges, the works. A smart kid. Sergeant Jack knew him from a youth center, then Morton got into drugs and car theft. When Morton got off Riker's Island, Jack found him a job lifeguarding at a swimming pool. The kid vanished two weeks ago. Just disappeared. Nothing unusual in that, is there?"

"I wouldn't know."

"Oh, that's right. Things like that don't happen to Gypsies."

The bitterness was strange in Isadore. Across the walkway, a pair of detectives searched for bloodstains with paper and benzidine. If the paper turned green or blue they scraped up the spot.

"Someone who knew Morton saw him get out of a car last night and run away from three white men. That was on the Manhattan side of the bridge, where the swimming pool is. It's deserted at night, except for junkies. Morton probably had the hot shot in the neck and the other in the arm when he started running. It's amazing he got so far. He had to climb over the barbed wire blocking that end of the bridge, beat the others across the bridge and scramble over this barricade. I suppose he went down to the river by then because he wasn't able to run uphill anymore."

One of the men on the abutment pulled the hanging rope in and began cutting stained threads from it.

"They could have just let him hang from that until he dropped, but I bet they didn't," Isadore said.

"Didn't his family miss him?"

"His sister's too busy working and his brother dropped off this bridge a year ago. There are no Hungarian fairy tale castles around here."

The small body was zippered into the bag and started its trip to the van. Isadore rocked back and forth against the rail chewing his lip until he dug a fresh stick of gum from his pocket.

"You know, I have this funny reputation for reading."

The sound of excited children interrupted Isadore as they swarmed around the police loading the van.

"Reading about Gypsies instead of arresting them, for example," he went on. "So when the commissioner stuck me with the crown, thanks to you, I went to the library to read up on it. Only, the Army archives I found there had the interesting pages cut out."

He took an envelope from the inside of his jacket. As

he sifted through the papers inside, Roman saw neatly written notes about photography. The detective found what he wanted, pages torn from a book, and held them out by the corners for Roman to read.

"Report of the 7th Army Interrogation Center: On May 7, 1945, an ancient box was delivered to Major K. of the 7th Army Intelligence Center by Hungarian Army Col. P. and twelve guards of the Hungarian Army. Col. P. said the box contained the Holy Crown of Saint Stephen. P. added that he must remain with the crown as he was the official custodian and guardian. P. stated that the keys were originally distributed to three people and that they were all now with Prime Minister Szollosi. A search for the keys was initiated. On July 24, Lt. G. of Intelligence arrived with the keys and the box was opened. It was empty."

Isadore turned the page over.

"P. was brought to the center and interrogated. P. explained that the crown, scepter and orb had been removed and buried. He then volunteered to go after the crown with Lt. A. of Intelligence. Maj. K. refused this request until permission could come from Intelligence HQ. However, on the following day, Col. P. and Lt. A. returned to Maj. K. and reported that they had fetched the crown during the night. An old, mud-covered gasoline drum was brought in and Col. P. chiseled the top open. Three very muddy and deteriorated leather boxes were removed. The boxes were falling apart. The crown, scepter and orb were carried to the bathroom, where the dirt was washed off by Col. P. and Maj. K. They placed them on the floor to dry and then put them back in their original chest. On Aug. 3, the box was reopened and the objects packed in bath towels. They were then replaced in the chest and the chest sealed with wax bearing the imprint of the dog tags of an American lieutenant who was present. Maj. K. states that he has never been able to discover where the crown was buried when it was in the gasoline drum."

Roman put his hand out for the rest of the envelope. Isadore shrugged and gave it to him.

"That was from the book I read. Boyle found all this

stuff scattered around the bridge. We already did a nin-
hydrin test on the paper, so we know the fingerprints
check with Morton's. Now, why was a seventeen-year-old
kid from Harlem ripping up books about the crown? And
why was he killed?"

"I have no idea," Roman said. "But you can start at St.
Patrick's." He held the paper against the bright sun so that
Isadore could see the watermark of a dove with an olive
branch. "It's the church's stationery."

CHAPTER
15

AT 100TH STREET, Isadore switched his siren on. The police car slewed through reluctantly parting traffic. The normally cautious detective ran his car half on and half off the road, shouldering cabs aside whenever he leaped away from an approaching light standard.

He turned onto Second Avenue and plunged through its truck traffic. When he turned right at Fifty-third, he cut the siren but not his speed until they were within a block of the church. He parked in a loading zone and they ran to St. Patrick's.

The patrolman outside the north transept greeted them nonchalantly, and inside the Hungarian guard waved them past the metal detector.

"A Gypsy rushing to church?" he joked.

Their steps reverberated through the empty cathedral. Reggel was in the sanctuary.

"I almost didn't wait for you," he yelled and jiggled his keys in the spotlight. "Isadore too? What zeal. And a red face like an Irishman. The church is affecting you."

"Like some halvah?" Isadore asked tersely when he reached the bay.

Reggel slapped Roman on the back. "When this is over I'll invite both of you to Budapest. You'll be heroes."

He opened the double doors and they descended into the crypt. Csonka rose from his chair beside the chest and went to guard the bay.

Reggel began unlocking the chest. His good-natured chatter reached Roman and Isadore no more than the sound of a running faucet. Reggel undid the last padlock and pulled the lid open.

Orb, scepter and crown reflected the crypt's fluorescent light.

"Why do you two look surprised?" Reggel laughed. "Here."

He picked up the cushion bearing the Holy Crown and gave it to Roman.

Roman returned the cushion to Reggel and carried the crown closer to the light. His eyes flitted over kings created with naïve, staring faces, over miniature posts carrying pearls individually formed and impossible to imitate, and finally to the distinctly awry cross. The Hungarian let the cushion hang in one hand and shook keys impatiently in the other. Roman turned the crown over to look inside.

"I suppose he deserves to have a close look," Reggel conceded.

Roman finished his examination.

"It's the wrong crown."

Reggel flushed. The last of Isadore's saliva suddenly disappeared from his mouth.

"Don't joke, Gypsy."

"No joke. It's the wrong crown. A fake."

He handed the crown back to Reggel.

"You're crazy. There's no way anyone could get in here." Reggel hit the face of a burial vault. "There's nothing here but marble and bones. And Csonka was here all the time."

"I'm not talking about how it was done. I'm only saying that's a copy. For all I know, you've got the real Holy Crown at your mission."

Reggel put the crown back in the chest and rushed out of the crypt.

"Where is he going?" Isadore asked Roman.

"To get Dr. Andos, I suppose. He doesn't want to believe me."

"He's bigoted."

"No. He's scared."

All the weight of the church seemed to descend on Isadore.

"He's not the only one. I'd better stall the ushers and call the commissioner."

"Call the cardinal first," Roman suggested. "He got us into this."

"This is the real crown," Andos said as soon as he arrived in the crypt. Killane accompanied him, and the burial vault was full. "This is the same crown I examined last night and put in the chest, the same crown given to Saint Stephen a thousand years ago. Whose word are you going to take?"

"A Gypsy's, but not mine," Roman said. He took the crown, handling it like a piece of costume jewelry. "The real crown was handed over to the American Army by a group of Hungarian officers at Maltese, a bathing resort near Salzburg. Am I right, captain? Some things have never been explained about the transaction, such as why the crown was missing from the chest when that was first delivered."

"It's no great secret that it was," Reggel said.

"But it is a secret why it was hidden in an oil drum near a concentration camp for Gypsies. There was a young Hungarian officer who spoke Romany who took one of the Gypsies to the crown because the crown had had some rough treatment and had to be repaired before it was handed over to the enemy."

"I've got to call the commissioner," Isadore interrupted. "Get to the point."

"Let him talk," Csonka said from the corner. They were the first words anyone had heard from him. He stared at Reggel.

"The Gypsy was a goldsmith. The crown was broken, the top bows removed from the diadem. The officers had the clips to fasten it back, but they were afraid of trying to work the old gold. He did it for them, heating the gold and

joining the halves together. But there was a clip missing for
the left side, so he had to do with only one there. The Holy
Crown that arrived here had just one. You can see for
yourself, this crown has two."

The crown shook as Andos examined it again.

"Afterward, the officer who spoke Romany was given
the task of killing the Gypsy so no one would know it had
been tainted by his work. For some reason, the officer didn't
have the heart for it. He only shot him in the arm and told
him to lie still until they left."

"He's lying. He's making it up."

Roman took the crown back from the protesting doctor.
Before they could stop him, he had cut out a sliver of gold
with his penknife.

"Here." He gave it to Isadore. "Have your laboratory
examine it. When this crown should have been made, goldsmiths used crucibles of white clay. A modern forger may
melt down old coins, but he uses a graphite melting pot.
You'll find traces of graphite in this."

Andos covered his face. Killane put his arm around him,
less for comfort than support.

"I'll have Monsignor Burns take him to my residence."
He turned to Roman. "I'm surprised at how cruel you can
be."

"You'll find I wasn't."

Killane was skeptical. He walked Andos out of the crypt.

"The crown is out of the city by now, unless it's holed up
with Freedom Fighters in Yorkville. We'd still have a
chance then," Isadore reassured Reggel. "It's a pretty tight
neighborhood, but we can find the crown if it's there."

Reggel was amused.

"Very good, sergeant. You search your Freedom Fighters. In the meantime, my friend and I have a plane to catch
to Budapest. You can tell your police to open the doors.
We'll be out of the way."

"We can't open it up, not until the field examiners have
a chance to check all the prints, including Csonka's. He's
the only live suspect we have."

"Not necessarily."

No one had expected Killane's return. He stooped, reentering the crypt. In his black cape and red skullcap he looked like an ancient bird of prey.

"If Dr. Andos didn't know one crown from the other, it's just as likely he brought the false crown here last night. Which means that it could have been stolen any time during the day."

"Your Eminence," Isadore sighed, "during the day the crown was in plain sight of thousands of people. No one came near it then."

"Captain Reggel, was anyone close to the crown during the day?" Killane asked.

Reggel's eyes meandered over the panels etched in gilt.

"Of course," he laughed. "You and the priests. During the mass you were all around it."

"Where can we find the priests?" Isadore asked.

"I've already inquired about that. I've also had Monsignor Burns tell your officers there's been a breakdown in the lighting system but that the doors would be open soon. You can put the crown on display whenever you want, Mr. Grey."

"A fake? Why?"

"Because, even if the priests did steal the crown, they couldn't leave with it. According to Captain Reggel's orders, they were searched with a metal detector. The Holy Crown is still with us, probably hidden in the sacristy or near a door. And whoever made the switch will have to come back for it.

"Correct me if I'm wrong, sergeant, but it is true, isn't it, that if the crown is gone from St. Patrick's you won't find it by roadblocking airports but as a result of information, a tip? In other words, raising a hue and cry would be little aid to finding the crown if it is gone and no aid if you want the thieves to return and lead you to the crown here. Time is a consideraion, isn't it?"

"Your Eminence, you could talk me into fish on Friday," Isadore congratulated him. "But priests stealing the crown and leaving it in St. Patrick's? How long do you think I'd last in this Police Department if I came up with a story like that?"

"How long will you last if you say the crown is not in the church? If the Hungarians didn't take it and it is gone, there's only one man who could have taken the crown out without being searched. Me."

"There is a certain logic to that."

After Killane left, Isadore and Reggel searched the ambulatory, the sacristy, anywhere the crown could be hidden. A breathless Monsignor Burns joined them.

"The fathers who came from Chicago to say evening mass yesterday? I located them in Chicago. They never left and they were never here. They even say I called them three days ago and told them not to come. There's something else, a small thing that probably means nothing. I wouldn't mention it if the situation weren't so—"

"Mention it," Isadore said. "Please."

"One of the maintenance men didn't show up for work today. Not that it's unusual, you see."

Isadore interviewed the chief of the maintenance crew, who identified Morton's picture.

"Tell me," Isadore asked Burns. "The boy who worked here, would he ever be able to find out these priests' names and where they could be reached?"

"The list was posted in the sacristy, names and churches." The monsignor's jaw hung elastically. In front of the high altar Roman was finishing the arrangement of the crown on its stand. "I thought the Holy Crown was stolen."

Reggel's hand gripped Burns' arm in a vise.

"The Holy Crown is not stolen. Do you understand—the crown is here."

CHAPTER 16

"THERE WEREN'T GOING to be any special viewings."

"Captain Reggel." Nagy rolled a fat, unlit Cuban cigar between his fingers. He stroked his stomach with a pudgy hand adorned by a pinky ring of amber and gold. "Captain, we can afford to be generous now. I won't hear any more protests. Let the American scholars look at the Holy Crown. It will be the last chance they ever get."

At the door he stopped.

"And one more thing, captain. The Gypsy the cardinal employed. Keep him away from the crown when the Americans come. It makes a bad impression."

"That's it then," Reggel said when he returned to Roman. "And if the man from the Metropolitan Museum is as good as you say, he'll spot the fake from the last pew."

St. Patrick's evening mass was over. Patrolmen and Hungarian secret police guarded a church that was empty except for the three men and the fake.

Isadore led the way to the radio in the bridal room. He picked up the receiver once and put it down.

"That's all he said?" he asked Reggel. "Nagy didn't get a call about the crown?"

"We can't find the crown. What does a call matter?"

"How much could they ask for the Holy Crown? A million dollars? Ten million? You don't sit on a ransom like that. If you have the crown, you call. God, you can imagine what we'd be willing to pay, let alone the Hungarians. If you have the crown."

"Call the commissioner," Roman urged Isadore. "You're thinking too much."

The Gypsy was not being sarcastic.

"Yeah, sergeants aren't supposed to think, I know," Isadore murmured. "Run scared, cover yourself. The Jew blew the Holy Crown."

He snatched the receiver. An electronic bark answered.

"This is Detective Harry Isadore at St. Patrick's. Get me five men from the bomb squad and a pair of field examiners. No fuss, just send them over."

Isadore let the receiver drop back into its cradle.

"The squad can find anything. I figure they'll say something if they come up with a crown."

Roman shook his head. "It's not worth it, Harry."

Isadore leaned back in the gilded bridal chair. The Gypsy had never called him by his first name before.

"You made this my case, Roman. Now, what can you do about the crown?"

Roman and the fake were gone when the bomb unit arrived. Isadore set the field examiners to work spreading fingerprint powder over the altar with generous turkey feather dusters. Once they were hard at work, he stole a small hammer from their kit.

A new shift of Hungarian guards and patrolmen arrived. Reggel joined Isadore with two of the Hungarians, who had red ears and blanched faces.

"Something new," Reggel reported. "These heads of lettuce have just informed me that while they were on duty about an hour after last night's mass the priests returned. The priests were here for maybe half an hour. That was before Csonka's shift. They claim they searched the priests thoroughly before letting them leave."

It was then Reggel's turn to watch the detective weed out the patrolmen who had been on duty after mass. Isadore found his men cracking gum outside the transept door. Their conversation didn't reach Reggel until Isadore became agitated.

"Why not?"

"Because they were priests," one of the patrolmen answered defensively.

"And if the Cardinal Hayes marching band showed up, would you let them in, too?"

"Things are really falling apart," Isadore admitted when he returned. The two men sat in a pew. Like dark, armored mice, the bomb squad slipped in and out of chapels.

"Five priests returned with an excuse about forgetting something in the sacristy. They had a note supposedly signed by Burns, but his stationery seems to be turning up everywhere lately."

"My man on the sacristy steps never saw the priests."

"Once they were inside, nobody did. Until the priests left."

"They came for the crown without taking it?"

"Your men had the metal detector," Isadore said. "Am I cutting my throat because they did a sloppy job?"

"No. I would cut their throats if they did."

The phrase was not figurative in Reggel's mouth.

"Okay. At least now we know the crown was here to come back for. The priests must have moved it." Isadore took a church pamphlet from his jacket and opened it to a floor plan of St. Patrick's. He penciled X's where the Hungarians had been stationed and from the X's drew fields of vision.

"Csonka and the man on the sacristy steps could see the bay, period. The others, at the transept doors, could see the transept area, the communion rail and the front pews. Columns would block off everything else. The priests had more than stolen stationery; they must have had Morton's keys. So they had nine-tenths of St. Patrick's to hide the crown in."

The bomb squad worked its way to the front of the

church. So far no one had searched the galleries, boiler
room, the forest of pipes in the organ loft or the spires.
What if Quasimodo had something to hide, Isadore wondered.

"Sergeant Isadore!"

Not Quasimodo but Commissioner John Lynch strode
into the church. At his voice, the bomb squad froze as if a
director had called a halt on a movie set.

"There's a bomb here and you didn't call me?"

"It's a little more complicated than that."

Isadore and Lynch huddled beside a confessional. As he
listened, Lynch combed his hair feverishly with his hands.

"Could you show me the crown you do have?" he
whispered through his teeth.

The two men marched along the communion rail toward
the Gypsy.

"And what the hell are you doing?" were Lynch's first
words to Roman.

The maintenance room Roman worked in was a leftover
hole in the wall opposite Killane's private sacristy. Cans of
putty littered the floor around a sink and an oven used for
melting the old wax out of votive candles. On the drainage
surface of the sink sat one box of green vitriol and another
of salt. Roman was using the hammer Isadore had stolen to
beat on the inside of the crown.

"It's the commissioner," Isadore explained and hoped
Roman had an answer.

"Trying to—" Roman began when Lynch pulled the
hammer from his hand.

"Beautiful, sergeant. You lose one crown, and by the
time I find out, you're tearing apart a second one. Is it
possible you're insane? Hand over the crown," he ordered
Roman.

"Will you listen to him, commissioner?"

"The only person I want to talk to now is the cardinal,
as soon as I've cleared out your menagerie. Where's that
Hungarian?"

When Reggel squeezed into the room, Lynch gave him

the crown and reported what he'd found happening to it. Reggel handed it back to Roman.

"Are you crazy, too?"

Reggel gestured for Roman to speak.

"I'm trying to buy us some time before word gets out that the Holy Crown is stolen. Sergeant Isadore thinks the longer this can pass as the real thing, the sooner the thieves will feel safe about coming back for the Holy Crown. There are going to be some men here tomorrow who won't be easy to fool. So I'm doing a little restoration work on it."

"With a hammer?"

"I don't know how sharp your eyes are, but if you had a magnifying glass you'd see hammer marks on any piece of crown jewelry. The trouble is that each century the tools of goldsmiths change, hammers included. The peen marks on this crown are wrong by eight centuries. I filed the face of the hammer you're clutching so it would leave the appropriate marks."

"In other words, you're improving on the forgery."

"You grasp the concept."

Score one for the Gypsy, Isadore gloated in the pit of his soul.

"What else have you got planned?" Lynch demanded and waved to the warming stove.

"The color's off, one of the clips has to be taken out and the whole thing could use a cleaning to look better. It might work."

Lynch threw the hammer down on the sink.

"I don't see any well-equipped laboratory around here for all that, but the real problem is the real crown is probably a thousand miles away from here by now. Isn't that most likely the case, sergeant?"

"It's possible."

"Possible? I saw your fake bomb scare out there. We'll know pretty damn quick if the crown is here." Lynch wrung his hands, getting a hold on himself. "Sergeant, I'm going off to see the cardinal. You stay here. If that antique dealer touches the crown again, shoot him. Then you can shoot yourself."

When Lynch was out of earshot, Roman picked up the hammer and resumed work.

"Sit down," he told Isadore. "It's going to be a long night."

Isadore closed his eyes. "I think I should have called him sooner."

Roman tapped the hammer over the gold.

"Killane always wanted it in God's hands. Now He's got it."

Wearily, through slit eyes, Isadore watched Roman refashion the fake. One large brown hand cupped the gold bows, the other hammered steadily, with casual familiarity, the hammer head slapping down to make the faintest possible impress. All the Gypsy's tension was in his fingers, fingers that constantly turned the oversized crown, and palms that polished the stones with their sweat of concentration.

Isadore pushed himself off the bucket to check the vitriol in the oven. The liquefied crystals were starting to harden.

"Your apprentice is coming down with sunstroke." Isadore undid the top two buttons of his shirt.

Roman glanced in the oven.

"It's coming along fine. Take it out and put in a plate of incense coals. You'll find some in my jacket."

"You plan to sleep here?" Isadore held up a toothbrush he found with the coals.

"If you don't tell on me, I won't tell on you."

Inside the cardinal's residence, Commissioner Lynch was long past remembering that its second name was the Powerhouse. The power sat behind his desk, unfatigued.

"Have you made your choice, commissioner? The priests, the Hungarians or me?"

"Accusing yourself doesn't help me find the Holy Crown; it just stops me."

"Then say you accuse the Hungarians, which you have to if the crown is gone and I didn't take it from St. Patrick's. I can tell you what would happen. Diplomatic relations would be broken and cultural exchanges will end. American tourists will be arrested on fraudulent charges in

Hungary and other Central European countries. There will be a motion for condemnation in the United Nations. The Vatican, which sponsored the crown's return, will be very embarrassed. In the end the United States will pay millions in reparations. Which won't stop our friends the priests from returning at their leisure and removing the crown from St. Patrick's."

Lynch tried the high road. "We should be working together instead of threatening each other. Here we are, heads of the two biggest Catholic organizations in the country, fighting. Your Eminence should cooperate. I don't second guess you on spiritual matters; you shouldn't interfere in criminal investigations. Do you mind if I say that right now you're using blackmail?"

"Not at all."

"I gather as much. Then do me this favor. If I can punch a hole in this story about the priests hiding the crown, will you let me put out a bulletin? Good. Now, five men go helter-skelter in St. Patrick's around six of Reggel's secret police." Lynch leaned over the desk. "The floors of the church are stone. The men wore shoes, not sneakers. How in the world did the Hungarians miss hearing them?"

Killane pressed a button on his intercom and asked for a fresh pot of coffee.

"You need it," he told Lynch. "They took off their shoes, of course."

Roman spread live coals over the vitriol and gave Isadore the task of fanning them.

"You're doing a wonderful job," Roman said. "Have you had any experience at this?"

"Will I need it where I'm going?"

The vitriol burned to a rosy hue. Roman let it cool, then ground it to dust with the hammer, adding salt as he worked.

"There's nothing more I can do for you?" Isadore asked politely before returning to his nap.

"Wine and a feather."

The detective rubbed the pouches under his eyes.

"The wine I know they got. The feather?"

He fetched a cup of sacramental wine and a small camel's hair brush.

"Courtesy of the field examiners. I might as well hang myself completely."

Roman added the wine drop by drop until the vitriol powder liquefied. He painted the preparation carefully around the crown's diadem of red gold. Isadore sat on his bucket and pondered dully how much practice the Gypsy had at this sort of labor in the rear of his antique shop.

"Tell me the truth, Roman, how do you manage to produce whatever your customers want?"

"The truth, sergeant, is told only in Romany."

After a fashion, Isadore had to admit, the answer made sense. He undid the buttons of his shirt while Roman put the damp crown in the oven. Sleep continued to weigh down Isadore's eyelids. He reached into his jacket for another No-Doz. His hand came out dripping from a melted bar of chocolate halvah. A brown stain was starting to spread to the outside of the jacket.

"Some days. . . ."

A wisp of smoke trailed from the dried crown when Roman removed it from the oven. He washed and scrubbed it with the toothbrush, then returned it to the oven. After a minute he removed the crown again and wrapped it in church linen to cool.

At a knock on the door, Isadore wiped his hand and buttoned his shirt. He slipped out of the steaming room to face the chief of the bomb squad.

"Nails, coins, a fingernail clipper. No bomb. Do you want me to tell the commissioner?"

"Aren't there nonmetallic bombs?" Isadore stalled.

"Gelatine, sure. We would've found it if it was here. We even looked in the cameras in the baptistry."

"Cameras?"

"Yeah, the cameras the Hungarians confiscated."

Isadore was already running down the aisle.

Reggel reached the bell tower of the north spire. He smashed open its locked door by using the handle of a metal detector as a spear. The beam of his flashlight played over the nineteen bells. The largest, named St. Patrick, weighed three tons. The smallest, St. Godfrey, was smaller than a man. In the dark the bells looked like gross, flourishing nightflowers.

And the night was only half over.

CHAPTER 17

THE SMALL WATCH stood boldly in the middle of Killane's desk. It was 2 A.M.

"If the crown was stolen from the crypt, it has now been gone for twenty-four hours," the cardinal reported. "Twenty-four hours to be anywhere. If it isn't in St. Patrick's, you won't find it tonight or in a week or even a month."

"Is that true?" the deputy mayor asked Lynch. He had left his own advertising agency to run the mayor's election campaign. In essence, his duties were to help his employer survive to run again. Since he had arrived within minutes after Lynch called him, sleep still puffed his face and matted one side of his razor-cut hair.

"Of course, it's true. The crown was stolen at least twenty-four hours ago. The only controls we have over travelers is at the airports, and amateur hijackers get through those all the time."

"Have you got the art theft squad on this?"

"There is no art theft squad. A plainclothes team worked on the Star of India theft ten years back, but they were split up in the reorganization."

The deputy mayor poured some more coffee and allowed himself a rare cigarette.

"Just what is our culpability in this, Jack?"

"The Hungarians were responsible for whatever happened inside St. Patrick's, but the overall responsibility is still ours."

"And this Hungarian captain in charge, he wants us to play along and pretend the crown's not missing."

"Because he's crazy on the subject—even I can see that."

"That isn't the point." The deputy mayor thought of his mayor sleeping happily in the Chilean alps. "The point is that the Hungarians had the responsibility for the Holy Crown when it was stolen. Once we turn down his request, the responsibility switches to us. But you don't think our odds on finding the thing are very good."

"Because I think this story about the priests is a lot of bull. I don't care if each had four arms, you don't steal a crown in front of five thousand people."

"Then it was the Hungarians or me," Killane concluded.

The deputy mayor screwed his cigarette out, turning it long after it was dead.

"You say the sergeant over there found some film in some cameras that were confiscated. How long before they're developed?"

"An hour before we get them back here."

"An hour," the deputy mayor repeated, rubbing the hollow of his collarbone. There hadn't been time to put on a tie. "I'd rather just leave it to the Hungarians and we could look as if we were doing them a favor by doing nothing. But you're right, Jack. If the crown's not here, we have to start looking someplace else. This is absolutely one administration that's not going to interfere with the police." He ducked the cardinal's look. "Well, you can wait an hour. If you don't find the crown here by then, go ahead. In the meantime, I'd better leave before the reporters get wind I'm here and start asking me why the mayor has to vacation in a Communist country. I told him not to do that."

Inside Roman's makeshift workshop, the fake crown lay dry and uncovered on a linen square. Roman worked at the sink, grinding charcoal into fine powder that would give the crown its final cleaning. The door opened and closed, and by the tread he could tell Isadore had returned. The detective stared ruminatively at the crown.

"I don't see any difference. Of course, I'm no expert," he added.

Isadore leaned against the wall with his elbow, his head resting on his hand. Roman sifted the black dust through a damp cloth. The Gypsy wrung the water out, wadded the cloth into a pad in his fist and began rubbing the crown.

"You know, Roman, there's another theory that occurs to me. Say a criminal is hired to help take care of a crown because he knows a lot about this sort of royal jewelry. During the exhibit, he arrives and claims the real crown is gone and a fake was put in its place. He even cuts off a piece from the crown and the gold has something in it it shouldn't have. Only the criminal doesn't really cut the sample from the crown, he just pretends to and hands over a piece that was already in his palm. Once everyone is convinced, they let him work on this crown. They think he's making a fake more like the real crown, when what he's actually doing is making the real crown look like a fake."

Roman washed the charcoal off the crown and dried it.

"Why would he do that?"

"People don't guard fakes as well as real crowns. Pieces of evidence get lost all the time and nobody gets excited. Then if it gets back to the man with the magic hands, all he has to do is a little restoration and, presto, the Holy Crown reappears. It just takes a smooth operator and a little patience. What do you think of my idea?"

The Gypsy hammered a white powder out of the chalk sticks.

"It's as good as anything else I've heard."

"That's all you have to say?"

"Would you like to know what's really funny about your idea?"

As Roman talked, he rubbed the chalk dust over the crown, giving it an almost blinding shine.

Reggel placed the fake on Killane's desk. It was 3 A.M. and the films had not arrived.

"I'm afraid I've failed," Killane said. "Captain, would you please call the ambassador and tell him the situation?"

"We're not even going to wait for the films?" Isadore asked. "Why not?"

Lynch didn't answer and Isadore leaned on the phone.

"Get away, sergeant."

"You can listen for two minutes." Isadore pointed at Lynch. "Go ahead, Roman. Tell them what you told me."

"All I said was that once you start your spectacular dragnet there won't be any Crown of Saint Stephen or any *sanctissima corona*, not even if you get it back without a scratch."

"Explain that," Killane demanded.

"You thought I was cruel to Andos. Sergeant Isadore thought I made a slip when I said the hammer marks on this crown were off by eight centuries instead of ten. I wasn't. The Holy Crown of Hungary is a fake." Roman smiled. "No, I don't mean the crown on the desk. I mean the Holy Crown that everyone is so eager to get killed for. Look."

Reggel tried to protect the fake on the desk, but Roman grabbed it away.

"This fake is good enough to show you. Andos said the top half was from the original crown and the bottom belonged to King Géza. Now, gentlemen, use your eyes."

Roman stepped around Lynch and placed the crown on the commissioner's head. It sank down to Lynch's mouth.

"Your head's not that small, commissioner. The crown wasn't made for Géza or any other man. It was made for a woman and it had to be big enough to accommodate her hair. The stones are a woman's: sapphire for chastity and pearls for modesty. Thank you." He took the crown off Lynch's head. "An ordinary woman's crown made at the royal workshop at Regensburg. There were probably fifty made like this in the twelfth century, a hundred years after Géza was dead."

"The top half is from Saint Stephen's crown, Mr. Grey," the cardinal reminded him. "That's what's important."

"That's the fascinating part, Your Eminence. The bows of red gold aren't from any saint's crown, they aren't from anybody's. Who knows what happened to Saint Stephen's or what it looked like? It disappeared after his death. But about three hundred years later, for political reasons or religious ones, someone decided to make a new crown. You can understand that anyone who could claim Saint Stephen's Crown had an edge on the throne. The problem was that he couldn't make his forgery out of a crown anyone would recognize and he couldn't have a new one made at Regensburg.

"His solution was ingenious. Nobody would recognize the ornamental gold bands from the cover of a Bible after they were bent into bows for Saint Stephen's crown. It wasn't the perfect solution because the flat bands had enamel plaques and the plaques suffered and the bands cracked when they were bent. But if you put a cross on top and attach it to a lady's diadem, what do you have? The Crown of Saint Stephen, the greatest fake in history. The forger hired for the job wasn't so successful, since he was killed when his job was done. When the Gypsies left Hungary for the rest of Europe, they carried the story that they had to travel because it was a Rom blacksmith who made the nails that crucified Jesus. There was another story that it was a Rom who made a crown from a Bible.

"So, start your fun and games, commissioner, but you better hope you fail. Because when the real crown is found, it's going to face more than the eyes of experts; there'll be authentication with spectrographs and carbon 14, and those tests are going to say the same thing I did. Then you'll find out that it's one thing to lose the Holy Crown of Hungary and another to tell the Hungarians that their most precious symbol is some medieval hoax, that it's worth no more than this fake—ten thousand dollars in gold and poor-quality stones."

The antique dealer, his face darkly in need of a shave and his shirt clinging with sweat, placed the crown elegantly in the center of Killane's desk. Killane and the rest looked with new eyes at the copy's crooked bows and off-center cross.

There was a knock at the door, and Isadore came back with the delivered films.

"It was a stall," Lynch said.

* * *

Isadore's catch consisted of black-and-white prints, slides and two 8-mm films confiscated on the second day of the display. Each was separately packaged according to the owner.

There were prints of unknown people blocking views of the United Nations, Radio City, Rockefeller Center and the façade of St. Patrick's. Waving. Mugging. One lone picture was of the crown in the sanctuary, but it was out of focus.

The slides introduced more anonymous faces. Hotel room views. A long-focus shot that turned Madison Avenue into a rolling snake. Suddenly a close-up of St. Patrick's front entrance, the Lily of the Mohawks in low-relief crazed and ecstatic. The Holy Crown seen between heads. A long-focus shot with the crown luminous as a painting by Caravaggio. Another with the sanctuary abruptly filled with priests.

"It's the evening mass, the right one," Isadore said. "Those are the phony priests."

"With a few thousand watching them." Lynch's voice came out of the dark with more interest than Isadore had dared hope.

A shot of a badly balding priest mounting the pulpit. The next shot was black and so were all the rest.

"Must have been when the camera was taken away."

Isadore put the slide machine on the floor and replaced it with a film projector. The lights went out again.

The scene was a hotel room and the actors were two young couples. The dominant color was flesh. One of the girls was a natural blonde. The action was nonstop. The viewers in the cardinal's office squirmed, though with none of the imagination of the performers.

"I guess this explains why this guy never picked up his camera," Lynch remarked. "Can you speed the film up a bit, sergeant?"

Isadore moved to the 16-mm gear.

"We took this in the church. There must be something from it," he hoped grimly.

Bodies parted and collided like two, three or four hands clapping. Mutely, endlessly. Roman resisted the impulse to ask what the North American record was. The prevalent

embarrassment warned him against it. There wasn't a
single frame from the church.

"I have to beg Your Eminence's pardon about that,"
Lynch said, adding that he thought the people were from
out of town. Roman glanced over at Isadore. Was it possible the commissioner concealed a sense of humor?

Isadore put the second reel of film on. At once they
were looking at the exterior of St. Patrick's. The camera
dwelt on each linden and elm planted on the sidewalk and
on the islands of grass beside the buttresses. Then they
were inside watching the priests enter the sanctuary. The
film was of surprisingly good quality using available light.
Crown and priests stood out clearly.

"Don't take his camera away," Isadore prayed.

The owner of the camera seemed to be trying to squeeze
the whole service into one reel, giving the viewer selected
highlights. Isadore knew the type, someone who put real
titles on his home movies. Mass moved briskly along, cutting from the sermon as soon as the priest opened his
mouth.

Communicants spread out along the rail. A priest raising the host. A chalice passed to the backs of heads.
Another priest bringing a full one.

"There! Run it back."

Lynch was on his feet.

Isadore put the film in reverse and started again at the
ciborium chalice being passed along the communion rail.
As the first priest carried his emptied chalice to the altar, a
second brought his full one forward. The camera veered to
the side and back to the sanctuary.

"What happened then?"

"Somebody pushed his arm," Isadore suggested.

"No," Reggel said. "I remember. There was an argu-
ment at the pamphlet counter. It was over in a second and
the man was thrown out."

"That's right," Isadore agreed. "He said he was short-
changed, but he admitted he was wrong when he got outside."

A third time, frame by frame. One priest going from the
rail and the other from the altar. The crown cut off from
view by two cross-emblazoned backs. A frame moving to

the side. The empty choir stalls. The transept. Choir stalls.
The approaching priest. The crown seen between the
priests, each a foot past on either side.

"Again. Can't you get it any bigger?"

Isadore moved the projector against one wall and the
screen against the other.

The film repeated to the same frame of the priests' passing. The elbows were those of the priest returning to the
altar, the fingers of his left hand on top of the chalice.

"What's he doing?"

"Covering the chalice with linen," Killane answered
Lynch.

"How long?"

"It's a little faster on film," Isadore said. "About two
seconds' worth of diversion. If anyone had been in the
choir stalls, they would have seen it."

"What about the people along the communion rail?"
Roman asked. "Why didn't they?"

"Haven't you ever seen people taking communion?" the
cardinal asked him in return. "Their heads are bowed or
looking up. One doesn't look ahead."

And once again. By now they could almost hear the
outraged shout at the rear of the cathedral, see the empty
chalice in the right hand move toward the crown, the silver
mouth engulfing gold, the left hand following with the
replacement, the screen of stiff, embroidered chasubles
parting to reveal a new crown and reassure the barely
alarmed eye. Reggel still stared after the lights went on.

"It took nerve," Isadore admitted ungrudgingly.

"Planning." The administrator had been replaced by
the cop in Jack Lynch. "God, imagine the planning."

He wandered to the cardinal's desk and looked at the
watch. It was 4 A.M.

"What did he need? Church plans, keys, a list of the
visiting priests."

"A dead boy," Isadore added.

"Impersonation and a simple diversion," Lynch concluded. "Everything thought out probably before the
crown ever got here. And it couldn't leave the church and
we can't find it. That's about as neat as you can get."

"Not that neat. He failed to run Reggel and me off the road," Roman observed.

"In the greater scheme of things, a small failure." Lynch shrugged.

"No. It means that Captain Reggel, of all people, was supposed to be put out of the way, and it makes me wonder why. And there's the mistake of the copy—not that it's a bad one, but that there is one at all."

The Hungarian turned from the screen.

"The copy, Reggel," Roman shook his head sadly. "Nobody can make one from pictures; you have to work from the real thing. But how could anyone if the Holy Crown has been locked up for a hundred years? See, that's the question you were supposed to ask, and you never have."

Reggel returned and sat in the chair opposite Roman. He put his hand out and Roman gave him his cigarette. The captain took a deep drag on it.

"So you think the time has come?" he asked.

"Come and gone."

Reggel handed the cigarette back.

"It's amazing. I've waited all this time, all this time, and I never recognized him." He was on the point of laughing. "The priest in the film, the one who stole the crown, is named Odrich."

Isadore was the first to react.

"Could you spell that for me?"

CHAPTER
18

"WHAT DID YOU want me to tell you? That I was a war hero of the Nazis? That of course I knew there was a copy, I arranged for it to be made by condemned Jews? Or just to watch out for my old friend, he's a murderer and a thief?

"How do you explain to Americans that Hungary owes nothing to them and never has? You took away three-quarters of our land after the First World War and wonder how we could have accepted the land back from Hitler. The rape of Czechoslovakia and Rumania? It was our land!

"The Germans asked for nothing more than thirteen divisions on the Eastern Front. I volunteered, eighteen-year-old lieutenant. I saw the Second Hungarian Army vanish between Voronezh and Stalingrad. Germans, Hungarians, Italians, Spaniards all vanished. I survived and they gave me some medals and sent me to a German company. That was where I met Eric Odrich."

"What was he?"

"The company commander, a captain at twenty-one.

An aristocrat like me, believe it or not. But he had been to school in England and, more important, to the Order Castles. You know the Order Castles?"

His answer was a blank response.

"Ah, well, the Order Castles were Hitler's version of the Teutonic Knights, with fencing and mountain climbing and, above all, study of the German race's right to rule the Slavs. A six-year course, and Odrich graduated in four. You see, he was a born leader."

Reggel paused to take another cigarette from Roman. Isadore stared coldly.

"During the disasters of that first retreat we became quite close. Eric was a compelling man. When they withdrew him from the front lines and sent him to the rear to enjoy the fresh air of the Alpine Korps, he took me with him. I stayed for a year, until Budapest started recalling every officer it could find to meet the Russians.

"We didn't meet again until the summer of forty-three in Budapest. From his uniform I thought he was with the SS, but he was a colonel in the Einsatzstab Reichsleiter Rosenberg. Rosenberg's group was safeguarding the artworks of Europe. In occupied countries like France this meant confiscation. But for an ally like Hungary, Odrich told me, he would only catalog and copy.

"I was a captain in the special guard assembled for the protection of the Holy Crown. He convinced me to persuade the rest of the special guard to let him make a copy. I even found the Jewish prisoners to do it, and he made them special artists of the Kuntschutz art institute. Just as other Kuntschutz artists had made a copy of the Louvre's Bayeux tapestry that was nearly indistinguishable from the original, the Jews would earn their freedom by recreating the symbol of the Hungarian nation. And so, while the war was busy being lost, our work progressed.

"Then, the retreat when the Russians encircled Budapest. Twenty boxcars of the great Hungarian works of art were dispatched to Munich. Odrich would personally lead us and the Holy Crown to a haven in Switzerland.

Who noticed in the rush that he had the Jews killed? That same night we left the palace in the last three armored cars of the Hungarian Army and two SS cars commandeered by Odrich.

"We didn't get far. The next day your planes strafed the road and destroyed one of the German cars. In the wreck was fifty thousand dollars in American money. My good friend, you see, was selling the Holy Crown. The Kuntschutz copy would go with us to Rosenberg, the real crown with Odrich to a buyer.

"This we learned when we surrounded his car. He tried to buy us off, and he convinced one member of the guard, a man named Martinovics, who was the younger brother of a well-known émigré in this city. Then your planes returned. Odrich, with both crowns, drove through us. I was the first one in a car to go after him. The planes followed both of us and we chased, the cars and the planes, over the roads.

"I don't know whether I hit him or the planes did, but his car overturned. We recovered the Holy Crown, the top separated from the bottom, and killed all the Germans and Martinovics. All but Odrich. He and the copy of the crown had disappeared. See, he was fooled. He took the wrong crown."

It was almost 6. A false dawn touched the windows and left a residue of blue. Reggel's voice was hoarse from cigarettes.

"Now, does that make you any wiser?" he asked.

"You should have told us before. It would have helped," Isadore said.

"How? He preached a sermon and I didn't know him."

"Why did you now, then?" Isadore persisted.

"When you made the picture larger," Reggel confessed, "I saw that triumphant smile."

Lynch broke into the reverie.

"Odrich kept the copy thirty years so he could steal the real one? What did he do in the meantime?"

"People find their callings. I became a policeman of

sorts. Odrich had some English schooling; he had taste. He was trained by the Nazis; he became an art thief."

"I never heard of him."

"Here you steal stock certificates," Reggel said tolerantly.

The phone rang. Killane answered it, then handed it to Lynch, who spoke for a few seconds and hung up.

"It looks like he got away with the real crown this time," he told Reggel. "The bomb squad swears there is no bomb or anything else in St. Patrick's."

His hand rested on the receiver ready to pick it up. There had been no calls to the deputy mayor or the mission and now there were no more reasons not to call. Second dawn hit the windows with a brightness that made their eyes water.

"Well, captain?" Lynch pushed the phone toward him.

"Fakes." Isadore watched the motes in the sunlight. "Everything is a fake. The crowns. Priests. The way the boy was killed. Why do we start believing them now?"

Lynch waited, holding the phone.

"Everything they do is a fake," Isadore said, "a diversion. And it works. We forget what we know is real. Odrich was at the mass and made the switch. He returns a few hours later for only one reason—he wasn't able to take the crown out before. He and his friends are in the church for half an hour and leave again. The next day we search St. Patrick's and can't find the crown. But why do we think it's gone? He had to walk out of the church in front of the same detector he passed a couple of hours earlier, and I know for real that if he could have gotten the crown through he would have done it the first time. The crown's not gone. We can't find it."

Lynch rubbed his eyes to cool them. At last, he put the phone down.

"It's your crown, Reggel. What do you want to do?"

"The Gypsy will fool the experts. We can keep the fake on display, and it will all seem according to plan."

"A police commissioner in my office all night will hardly

be according to plan," Killane pointed out. "Odrich must be keeping an eye on the church."

"I know, I know." Lynch picked up the fake crown and contemplated its saints. "Can you make something that looks like a bomb?" he asked Roman. "Can you find it?" he asked Isadore.

CHAPTER
19

ON THE OBSERVATION platform of the RCA Building, boys operated heavy, dime-fed telescopes like machine guns, creating carnage from Jersey City to Wall Street while parents counted their change. Roman stood alone.

The elevator opened and new sightseers poured out on the platform. A grinning Isadore was among them.

"You did it. They swallowed the fake."

"Really."

"Well, a couple of the experts said the crown almost looked too good. Maybe it's just as well you weren't there. Damn, you should have seen it, though. I was pretty proud. You going to come down now?"

"Why should I? I finally found the perfect hideout."

"From who?"

"You, until a second ago. And Reggel and the cardinal. I can't go home because Dany and Kore are there and I'm sick of lying to them."

A sea gull teetered in the updraft from the street one hundred floors below. Its wings were soiled and its head darted from side to side looking for scraps from the platform.

"Sergeant, did you know that Hungary has the highest suicide rate in the world? That's what Reggel's doing right now, and he's got you and Killane helping him. I don't want to."

"Suicide? We're dealing with a murderer. Here." He gave Roman a typed sheet of paper. It read:

"Erich Ordich, a.k.a. Eric Wilhelm von Odrich. Age: 54. Race: White. Nat.: German. Ht.: App. 5-11. Wt.: App. 175. Hair: Gray (?). Eyes: Blue (but may wear colored contacts). Speaks English with no accent. Also: Ger., Hung., Ital., maybe others. Military background: Wehrmacht. Einsatzstab Reichsleiter Rosenberg (ERR). ERR responsible for theft of artworks later located at Thuringia (also gold bullion), Werfen (Hungarian art train), Neuschwanstein, other sites. Still missing: 8,740 pictures, 423 tapestries, 634 marble sculptures, 1,096 bronzes (Repertoire des Biens Spolies Durant la Guerre 1939-45). Odrich reported missing in action, now considered residing in Italy under assumed name. Losses of Italian art today put at $10,000,000 per year. Most thefts from churches."

There were photos clipped to the paper, all from the communion movie. The largest was of a man in middle age as meek as an out-of-town priest could be, a face of sandstone rubbed free of half its hair and all individuality. The smaller photos were of the other priests, all younger men.

Isadore swiveled one of the telescopes up Fifth Avenue and dialed St. Patrick's into focus. Its architect had omitted one feature from the cathedral: flying buttresses. For that reason, St. Patrick's looked like a fortress. Even down the spine of the roof there rose a protective crest of gilded metal.

"That's nice." Roman handed the paper back.

"I made shorter ones up for the surveillance teams. Take a look."

Roman reluctantly took the detective's place behind the telescope and followed Isadore's finger.

"There are four teams for each side. One on the second floor of the archdiocese headquarters." Roman trained on the brownstone Vuillard mansions. "One above the French restaurant on Fifty-first Street." The telescope magnified a man reading a paper in the indicated window. As he turned a page Roman caught the glint of a rifle barrel. "One on Fifth in the Associated Press Building, and the last one in Saks on Fiftieth Street."

The dime ran out and the telescope clicked off.

"See, Roman, they've got to come back tonight or tomorrow. On Monday St. Patrick's gets its annual cleaning. There'll be industrial cleaners all over the place. Morton must have told Odrich about it, and Odrich can't take a chance the cleaners won't find it."

"You've figured it all out."

"I'll have the surveillance teams and four backup cars. Reggel and his men will watch the doors from the inside."

Someone had left half a candy bar beside the telescope. Roman broke off a piece and threw it in the air. The sea gull dropped like an elevator and snatched the candy in its beak.

"Sometimes for a Gypsy, you're a real wet blanket," Isadore complained.

Roman's laugh ruined his next throw. The gull squealed as the candy flew by out of reach.

"Okay, you've got this trap with a bait you can't find and a man who exists on paper. The problem is that the fake crown goes to Budapest tonight. It's going to be very suspicious that Reggel isn't on the plane. They're going to know why he wasn't by noon tomorrow. That'll be morning by our time. Reggel will be arrested at the mission and you'll be left explaining your story about the invisible crown to some much wetter blankets than me."

"If we can come up with the crown—"

"The hell with the crown."

Roman scored a bull's eye right in the gull's mouth.

"I have to keep Reggel alive. Do you think I took this job because of the Holy Crown? I'm just sorry I dragged you into it."

Isadore shrugged. "You know, Roman, I was just getting interested in it."

The detective left. Roman remained on the observation platform until the evening mass was over. A crowd formed in front of St. Patrick's to see the crown leave in its iron

chest. Ambassador Nagy himself directed the security
guards driving the cars from the Hungarian mission.

Roman stepped into the observation souvenir stand and
bought a cup of coffee. He took it out with him to the
south side of the platform and put a dime of his change
into a telescope. It came to life with the whirr of a time
bomb.

He sipped from the cup, then placed it on the wall.

The telescope lens climbed the tinted windows of the
Pan American Building to the roof. In a glass-enclosed
terminal, Nagy pushed patrolmen out of the way. The
terminal doors opened and the royal chest was carried out
to the waiting helicopter.

Roman watched the Hungarians enclose themselves in
the helicopter as its jet-powered rotors began turning.
Patrolmen clutched their hats, and the helicopter lurched
clear, more as if it were falling upward rather than flying.
Roman followed the helicopter until it vanished toward
Flushing.

Kore and Dany were waiting when Roman got home.

On the table were a newspaper article about the crown's
return and three boat tickets.

"We leave tomorrow, Romano, unless you've decided
to be a priest. In that case you don't need either of us."

"We are going, aren't we?" Dany asked.

"A Yugoslavian freighter. Five thousand Long Island
frozen turkeys and us. The Petulengro brothers have
stolen a car that was just polished."

Roman detoured the conversation by praising Dany's
supper, a dish of "poor man's caviar," cold eggplant and
garlic. "You ought to try some, Kore."

Dany poured Kore a beer. "Then we're not going," she
said. "If that's the case, some photographers called today
and asked me to take some assignments. What should I tell
them? That we've decided to stay?"

"I didn't say that."

"Are we going tomorrow or not?" Kore demanded.
"The Magyar crown goes back. What other reason is there
to stay? You don't even give reasons, you just wait

another day. We're not birds, you know. We don't fly someplace just because you do or stay because you stay."

"Then go." Roman pushed his plate away and stood up, a more astonishing act than Kore's histrionics because Roman never lost his temper. "Go do your posing and your driving, the two of you. I'm not the King of the Gypsies."

When they didn't go, Roman did.

Left alone, Dany and Kore looked at each other. She pushed Roman's plate over the table to the red-headed giant.

"Here, it'll just get warm."

After observing a period of offended righteousness, Kore unfolded his arms and picked up a fork. Dany found a pack of Roman's cigarettes and smoked in silence.

Roman walked south through Central Park. Leaves rattled as a wind picked up and cooled the park's nighttime population of muggers and bums. Roman passed through, undisturbed. A light rain washed the air.

The Gypsy had meant to walk until his anger at himself had cooled, but he found himself outside St. Patrick's and the rain was coming down harder. He tried one of the cathedral's front doors. It opened and he went in.

There was no sign of maintenance men or of Reggel's guards. It would be typical of the Hungarian, he decided, to put the men in confessionals. Next to the Chapel of the Holy Relics, a door to one of the gallery stairs was open. Nobody stopped Roman as he climbed them.

Rain muffled his steps while intermittent lightning illuminated the nave. Columns emerged and fell back into the dark. The thunder that followed made chandeliers creak, and far above the altar sooty cardinals' hats swayed. Roman moved to the organ loft more anxiously. The lightning was bright enough to reach into the confessionals and show him they were vacant.

The Gypsy's head snapped back as one arm went around his neck and another into his back.

He hit the gallery rail at his waist and grabbed the stone with his fingertips. A forearm as powerful as a man-trap twisted his head back farther. As Roman's fingers slipped off the rail, he kicked sideways and hooked one of the gallery's slender columns. The arm around his neck yanked him away and the paving of the church floor sixty feet below bobbed into view. He flailed outward with nothing to grab hold of.

"No," Roman tried to say, but the arm choked off his throat. Something new, cold as rain but hard, dug into his neck. The hammer of a gun cocked dryly beside his ear. As the barrel burrowed deeper under his jaw, the arm drew out of the way.

"It's me," Roman whispered. He grasped the molding along the top of the gallery to stop his plunge forward. "It's me."

He felt indecision, but the man's weight kept bending him forward.

"Pull me back, Reggel. You don't want to kill me."

The hammer slid by centimeters back into its bed. The other arm lifted Roman inside the rail and let go. He dropped on the gallery and rolled on his back. The first thing he saw was the gun still pointed at him.

Reggel appeared like the dark angel. His hair and clothes were black from crawling into the church's most inaccessible reaches, the wings of his cheekbones smudged moons under red eyes.

"What are you doing?" Roman demanded.

"Waiting to kill him."

"In the church?"

A bolt of lightning hit Madison Avenue behind the Lady Chapel's blue windows. Reggel's gun jumped at the flash and swung back to Roman.

"What you said about the Holy Crown itself being a fake—was that true or a lie?"

Roman watched the gun. Between the end of the barrel and the carapace was a molding like a wrinkle of flesh. He waited for the revealing flame. After a minute, the gun dropped and Reggel backed against the wall.

"I've decided you lied," Reggel told him.

Roman got to his feet. Blood that had been collecting with the immediate prospect of death flowed into his hands.

"Call it a theory, if you want," he said.

Reggel leaned farther into shadow.

"I did think you were Odrich at first."

"Then you realized you'd like to kill me, too. I know. The Magyar will out."

Lightning crossed Fifth Avenue and its thunder cut off Roman's words. During the pause he saw in Reggel an animal conserving its strength.

"Why are you alone?"

"Why not? In Hungary when they built a castle they used to leave a man imprisoned in its walls. This church claims me. As long as the Holy Crown is here I have to stay. Only I can't find the crown. I've looked everywhere. And if the crown is not here, the church still claims me."

"It could claim better."

"Ah." A note of rationality appeared in Reggel's voice. "You for one must be relieved."

"Churches don't claim Gypsies."

Someone else came in from the storm. It was a man without a raincoat. He propped himself against the fount of holy water and coughed violently until his lungs had wrung themselves out. From the fount, he moved to a bank of votive candles to warm his hands. The candles swarmed around him as a pyre and light reflected from him lit the chapel's mourning statues. Reggel was poised at the gallery rail as if he were going to launch himself out.

"When was the last time you slept?" Roman asked. "You're seeing things that aren't there."

"I'll see Odrich."

"If you happen to be raving at the right door. He has all the keys you do, he has four men and he knows where he's going. You'll be the lone protector of the Holy Crown, and they'll run right over you. If they have to," Roman added. "At the rate you're going, you'll be firing at ghosts."

"I'm not as crazy as you think. The church has to be empty so they can lead me to the crown. I'll kill Odrich, and the others will run."

Roman sat on the rail, making sure his back was firm against a column.

"You, Reggel, are a romantic."

The man below, no romantic, shook the poor box. Roman couldn't hear the box's report over the rain, but the assailant was discouraged. He wandered to the pam-

phlet rack and took pamphlets down with the zeal of a
convert. When he had an armful, he carried his booty to
a pew and pulled his trouser legs up. Two pamphlets went
inside each sock, half a dozen inside his pants and the
rest strategically placed within his shirt.

"For the warmth," Reggel explained. "We did exactly
the same thing with religious books in Russia. A good
Bible could stop a bullet."

Holding his armor in place, the visitor made a running
start for his dash from St. Patrick's. They heard his foot-
steps in the vestibule, the door opening and the rush of
rain inside.

"Now that you're here, stay. Keep me awake like the
ciganyi who played soldiers into battle."

Roman cocked his head. "Are you sure you aren't talking about cannibals?"

But Roman stayed. He and Reggel passed the rest of the
night talking on and off about the Gypsy's trip. Reggel
grew enthusiastic, as if he were going along.

"I will treat you to Budapest and we will stay on the
Buda side of the river." His face twisted with reminiscence
of the city. While he spoke, lightning danced from Rockefeller Center up Fiftieth Street. Roman couldn't help
glancing at the *son et lumière* of the colored windows.
On Saint Elizabeth's skirt of roses the black outline of a
linden leaf pressed against the glass abruptly, upside down
in the shape of a spade. It was gone with the next gust of
rain.

"What's the matter, Romano?"

"Nothing. What were you saying?"

Before Reggel could say, the church door opened again.
Kore walked in to the back of the pews, shaking rain off
his hat. Dany followed him.

"I'm going, Reggel," Roman said quietly. "So, tell me,
what will you do about your threat? What about the Rom
in Hungary?"

"There's nothing I can do anymore. The orders go
through. It would be different if I had the crown."

"I'll give you the Holy Crown for the Rom."

Dany and Kore looked around but failed to see the men
on the gallery.

"You're bluffing, Gypsy. You don't have the crown."

"But I know where it is. The ushers will be here soon. You can leave now and call Budapest from the mission. It will be an hour or so before the experts in Hungary know they have a fake. Retract the order and leave the rest to me."

"How will you know I do what you say?"

"I'll know. And if I'm wrong about the crown, you can always carry out your threat."

Dany was at the door. Kore uttered some exasperated grunts and joined her.

"Gypsy, tell me the truth. I want to believe you. When did you find out where the crown was?"

"You showed me, captain. When you tried to kill me."

CHAPTER
20

AT KENNEDY AIRPORT, Csonka took no chances about delivering his former chief to Budapest. Until their flight left he kept Reggel in the men's room sitting in a toilet cubicle. Csonka held a gun on him from the sinks and another security guard turned away interruptions at the door.

Two boys pushed their way into the lavatory, nevertheless. They were too busy fighting to pay attention to the Hungarians and their guns. Both boys were dark and as alike as brothers, but one was taller and he soon had his opponent on the floor. The one on the bottom screamed as if his life were in danger, although neither of Reggel's guards understood what was said.

In a superhuman effort, the smaller boy threw the larger one off. Locked together, they staggered into the guard at the door and accidentally knocked the gun from his hand. A foot kicked the gun through the door into the hall. The guard scrambled for it on all fours. He backed slowly into the lavatory, still on his hands and knees, as Roman brought the gun in. Reggel took Csonka's gun away.

"Do we get a gun?" Racki Petulengro asked.

"You get to drive the Magyar's car," Roman answered. "And this time he doesn't complain."

It was afternoon and young people were already bringing their blankets into Central Park for a music festival. Until it began they listened to rock on their radios. Nothing was said about a Hungarian crown on the news reports. The warm day turned into a clear night, and by the time the festival began there were 20,000 kids, hippies and what glossy magazines called "career couples" spread out over the grass. In Times Square, theatergoers of another generation sidestepped prostitutes and sneaked looks at peep shows. On the Harlem River boys swung on a new rope from the Highbridge.

In an office in the Saks Building across from St. Patrick's the phone rang. The detective at the desk turned down the second inning of the Mets against the Phillies on the radio and picked up the receiver. After a second, he turned the ball game off entirely.

His partner sitting in a dark adjoining office with a rifle and binoculars waited impatiently for the ball players to resume life.

The cop at the desk hung up.

"How do you like that? That was the Hungarian mission. They want us to arrest their security chief?"

"What for?" A response came from the dark office. "Anyway, he's got diplomatic immunity."

"There was something about him refusing to go back to Hungary. His own men are afraid to make the collar, so they want us to. That's a hell of a situation."

The partner finally appeared at the doorway with his rifle and a blank expression.

"They say he's in there"—the detective at the desk pointed through the blinds at St. Patrick's—"with Isadore. Isadore told us not to set foot in the church unless something popped. Now are we supposed to take orders from the officer in charge or from some Hungarians?"

"Call the commissioner and find out."

It was then 10 P.M., six hours after Roman had rescued Reggel.

Lynch was on Long Island for his daughter's wedding so

that he could use the mayor's summer cottage for a reception while the mayor was still in South America. The maid who answered the phone said the reception was over and the Lynches had gone with friends to a restaurant. The detectives took down the restaurant's number. It was standard procedure for the commissioner never to be out of reach of a phone, but Lynch was not at the restaurant.

Chief of Detectives Alvan Meyer answered his bedside phone at once. He was a big man with panda-sized worry circles under his eyes, and he told the detectives in Saks to stay where they were until he joined them. His wife helped him dress, but he lived on Staten Island and failed to arrive at Saks until midnight. With him was the commander of the Seventeenth Precinct. No one had been able to locate Lynch.

"Some time for him to disappear," Meyer observed.

Everyone knew the chief had been passed over for commissioner. He shuffled to a street map on the office corkboard. Eight red and blue tacks surrounded the block occupied by St. Patrick's.

"I thought the crown was back in Hungary."

"It is, but Isadore swears this German gang is going to hit tonight."

"Hit what?" Meyer picked up the Odrich fact sheet and read it through.

"Blue's surveillance around the church and reds are cars, unmarked with plainclothes." From nervous habit the detective explained the tacks on the map.

Meyer put the fact sheet down.

"Isadore thinks he's a goddamn historian. A gang is going to hit an empty church? Why isn't Isadore here if this is the command post?"

"I don't know. He wouldn't even take a radio with him."

"Sixteen detectives around an empty church." Meyer thrust his hands in his pockets. "And the Hungarian. What kind of trap is that?"

Meyer went into the darkened office and stared out the window. His first instinct was to go into St. Patrick's, apprehend the Hungarian and bawl out Harry Isadore. Not that he had anything against Isadore, but this was Meyer's first chance to embarrass Lynch. What held him back was in the corner of his eye, the little white palace of the cardinal. Killane could be the only reason Lynch would assign so many men for a futile surveillance, and there was a difference between embarrassing a commissioner and attacking a cardinal. The solution was to take personal command, make sure the Hungarian didn't escape and let the *Times* learn how many detectives were misassigned behind the back of their own chief.

"Shouldn't we at least try to reach the assistant commissioner?" the precinct commander inquired when Meyer returned. The chain of command went from Lynch to his assistant, and no one was more aware of the fact than Meyer.

"This is a plainclothes operation no matter who set it up," Meyer maintained. "If you want to help, you can sweep the area."

By 2 A.M. the only suspicious character picked up by the sweep was as officer from BOSSI. The Bureau of Special Services and Investigation had been watching Reggel on its own to update its own Hungarian-American file.

"Look," Meyer pleaded, "the Hungarian mission is phoning us every ten minutes to march in there and pick up their captain because he didn't take a plane today. What do you know about it?"

The man from BOSSI asked permission to call his headquarters before he answered. It took two minutes.

"Okay. We followed Reggel to the airport. He had a seat on Czechoslovak Airlines with a connecting flight to Budapest. He changed his mind, I guess, because he came back in town with some Gypsies and holed up in an abandoned apartment house on Houston Street. But why ask me? Detective Isadore was the one who picked up Reggel on Houston Street and brought him to the church. Ask Isadore."

"Isadore! That's why he didn't take a radio—so we couldn't ask him," Meyer burst out.

"Should we call the assistant commissioner now?" the commander suggested.

"No," Meyer rebuffed him. "We're going in the church. Get me the cardinal."

Meanwhile, like a defective orrery, the city continued to stir.

An IRT subway train broke down and stranded hundreds of the music lovers trying to leave the festival at the Columbus Circle station. Mounted police, unaware of the problem, tried to push the milling kids back in the station. Somebody knocked a cop off his horse with an accurately thrown bottle of apple wine, and quicker than one could say "The Grateful Dead" a small riot was brewing.

Similar difficulties were developing in Harlem. A liquor store was held up at gunpoint, and as the thieves ran, the proprietor followed them with his own unlicensed pistol. He killed one; only the people standing around Lenox Avenue weren't sure the white store owner had shot the right black man. Running inside, he locked all three locks on his door. The door and windows were permanently protected with wire mesh, so he felt reasonably secure until the window crashed in with a blast from a shotgun. Police cars were trying to converge on the scene, but neighborhood residents held them back with barricades of burning uncollected garbage. The people would have already burned out the store, but they were trying to figure out a way to get at the owner's liquor, too.

The detectives in Saks had barely put the phone down when it rang again. The assistant commissioner wanted to know where Lynch was and why Meyer was where he was. The Twenty-second Precinct requested more black plainclothesmen for Lenox Avenue. Central Park Command wanted all available men at Columbus Circle. And what about Reggel? the Hungarians demanded.

By the time Killane entered the office in Saks, Chief Meyer was on his way out.

"I just wanted to tell you, cardinal, we're going into St. Patrick's to take a man into custody. It's a Hungarian security officer who has no business there, and it's at the request of his mission."

Killane had taken the time to dress in his prince's cape. He laid it carefully over the arms of his chair so that it wouldn't bind when he sat. Meyer fretted at the door.

"I'm going over now," he emphasized.

"On whose authority?" Killane asked.

Monsignor Burns lit the cardinal's cigarette, cleaned an ashtray, set it by Killane and informed Meyer the cardinal was addressed as Your Eminence.

"Your Eminence, we've got a couple of riots tonight. I have to pull some of the men off surveillance here, so I have to take the Hungarian now. I haven't got time to talk about it."

"What has the man done?"

Meyer gave his wristwatch a labored gaze. The cardinal had taken thirty minutes to cross the street from his residence.

"Cardinal, Your Eminence, I got a complaint. I'm picking the man up. I'm canning the detective who's in there with him and then I'm going to go do my job like the city pays me for."

Killane was as unruffled as a spider on a web.

"Show me the complaint, Chief Meyer."

Meyer was thrown off stride. The use of his name reminded him that he was a Jew dealing with a Catholic cardinal and Catholic detectives were listening.

"See, this is a police watch in the church, Your Eminence. I don't need a written complaint to deal with unauthorized persons on police business."

"He's there on my authority."

"And the authority of the commissioner," Meyer shot back.

"Fine." Killane settled back for a long stay. "Let's wait for Commissioner Lynch."

Meyer was through for the moment and he knew it.

"All right, Your Eminence, I won't go in now because there are more important things to do. To do them I'm going to need every detective assigned to the church. With a little cooperation we could have worked something out. As it is, I'm very sorry."

Killane listened as Meyer ordered the detective at the desk to recall all the cars and surveillance teams.

"We can't reach Sergeant Isadore," Meyer said. "He will maintain the watch."

The detectives followed their chief's exit with their radio and rifle. The clergymen were alone.

"Your Eminence was grand," Burns applauded.

"Yes, so grand that St. Patrick's is now unprotected."

"What will you do?"

Killane looked at Burns in mild surprise. For once, the monsignor thought his cardinal had an answer.

CHAPTER
21

AT 4 A.M. the streets around St. Patrick's were as empty as the surveillance posts. The only vehicles parked were trucks owned by the industrial cleaners who would start working in the church early on Monday. Marked cars that regularly patrolled Fifth Avenue were on special duty at 125th Street and Lenox Avenue. Commissioner Lynch was with them at last, and the mayor had cabled a message of concern from Chile.

The doors of the middle truck opened and a man slipped out and crossed to the door set in the rusticated wall. He opened the door with a key of hard rubber so that it wouldn't complete the circuit of an electrical alarm. Four more men left the truck. Odrich, white stubble growing over the front of his skull, closed up the truck. Even if the surveillance team had remained at its post above the restaurant, it was unlikely they would have seen him. The rear of the truck was at an angle from the restaurant and the line of trucks cut off any view of the boiler room door.

Odrich took the lead inside the boiler room. All five wore black pullovers, black pants and tennis shoes and two carried nylon ropes fastened on their shoulders by epaulets.

At the far corner of the room, the first point where it was actually beneath the church, Odrich unlocked the door to a spiral metal staircase.

Isadore looked at the radium dial of his watch. It was 4:10. Nine hours had passed since he entered the priest's half of the confessional because Roman said it was the best place to watch the Holy Crown. Not that he could see the crown. But it had to be there, the detective thought, because there was no other place it could be, nowhere else as obvious and perfectly hidden. And it had to be there because Isadore was out of a job if it wasn't.

He glanced through the confessional grate at Roman. The Gypsy was asleep on the confessor's bench. Typical, Isadore told himself. He turned his weary attention to the panel at his feet. Every entrance to St. Patrick's was wired to it, and a red light would appear at as much as the insertion of a key in a lock. The panel was blank. Isadore rubbed his cramped legs.

The confessional facing Isadore across the nave was half open. There Reggel was at his post. Within the first hour he had slipped into the familiar hypnotism of the flickering candles. After eight hours the unsteady orange glow threw smiles on the faces of the marble statues staring back from their chapels, smiles of disinterested humor or the open mockery of those wearing their own crowns.

The pupils of Reggel's eyes blossomed in the darkness.

Isadore heard a scratch on the grate. Roman was awake and pointing up. Isadore listened, heard nothing and raised his eyebrows. The Gypsy pointed up again. Isadore looked at the panel. There were still no lights.

The detective shook his head. Besides pointing up again, Roman held up two fingers.

Sweat and adrenalin began circulating in Isadore. The silence didn't help. He opened his curtain far enough to see Reggel. The Hungarian was as still as a statue. Isadore opened his jacket, feeling for the revolver in his belt, then looked back through the grate.

This time Roman pointed to the other side of the sanctuary. Isadore took a final look at the electric panel. It was still dark. Well, fuck the panel, he thought and drew his gun.

There was no mistaking Roman's gestures anymore. Isadore drew the curtain back and looked straight at the gallery high along the south side of the sanctuary. At first he saw nothing but the gallery columns, and when something moved between them it seemed faint enough to be his imagination. The movement came closer and he could make out a head.

Odrich leaned confidently over the rail to survey the empty church.

Roman was not disappointed. The face in the gallery was lean and strong-featured, the partly shaven skull accentuating the high forehead. There were no lines of doubt and the pale eyes were serene. It was the face of a man fully conscious that in middle age he was more dangerous physically and intellectually than ever before. A face etched in silver.

Two younger faces joined Odrich's at the rail. The other priests, Roman thought.

One of them climbed the gallery rail. He balanced on it, then bent his knees and leaped out. Five feet into the open air he caught the chain of the chandelier. As the chain swung back to the gallery, the other of Odrich's assistants grabbed it and held it still. In all, they made no more noise than if the wind had brushed a window.

The man holding the chain pulled it closer to the wall. The one on the chain climbed it swiftly with the ease of a gymnast until he reached its base in the bay of the clerestory window a hundred feet above the floor. He rolled up the bottom of his sweater to uncover a wide belt equipped with rock-climbing straps.

The Alpine Korps, Isadore remembered.

From the gallery the chandelier chain was swung first one way and then the other so that the climber could fasten his straps to each side of the window's lead molding. His hands let go of the chain and he dropped no more than a foot, suspended by the straps across the face of the window where its stained-glass panels came together in stone trefoils.

On their own side of the sanctuary, Roman and Isadore heard the same soft landing of a body on a chandelier chain and the whisper as the chain was caught. The climber on the south window unbuttoned the coil of rope from his shoulder. Isadore looked across to Reggel's confessional.

Reggel had seen and heard nothing. Stone lips grinned at him secretively.

Hanging ten stories above the floor on each side of the sanctuary, the climbers seemed to have the power of flight. Their heads grazed the join of the window bays, and nearly within arm's reach were the great ribs of the ceiling meeting and radiating in three granite suns. They were far beyond where the police had searched, and Roman could understand why. Among the planes, medallions and ribs of the Gothic vision of heaven there was not one place in which to hide the Holy Crown.

The rope flew across the ceiling and was caught. Roman watched the man on the south window make his end of the rope fast through the clips on the window and assumed that the same was happening on the north side.

Odrich climbed the chandelier chain. If anything, he was faster and smoother than the younger man.

He touched the window perch like a bird reluctant to land. In one motion, he turned toward the rope stretched across the sanctuary and dove out.

A red light glowed on Isadore's panel, but the detective was no longer paying attention to it.

Odrich traveled hand over hand along the rope, his shadow swimming behind over the green ceiling.

The Gypsy was right, Isadore knew for sure now.

Odrich stopped in the middle of the rope, his feet dangling over the altar canopy. Above him in the last star of the ceiling was a dove. Hanging from the dove was a cardinal's hat.

There were four hats hanging from the ceiling, and they were all still, but during the storm there had been one stationary blood-red ring crossed by three swaying black rings. Roman had had a particularly good view of them while Reggel was pushing him off the gallery.

Odrich brushed the tassels out of his face and reached through the wires attached to the wide brim. As he lifted the hat's false cover a dull golden glow appeared in the dark.

Odrich carefully removed the Holy Crown by its cross.

Roman and Isadore pulled back the drapes of their booths. They saw no sign of Reggel.

Odrich swung his legs around the rope and held the crown tight to his chest with one hand. He just started back when every light in the cathedral went on at once.

Killane stood by the altar wing that controlled the lights. He had put on a chasuble.

"I order you to stop in His Name."

Isadore was out of the confessional, waving the cardinal back with both hands. The man on the south window sighted on Isadore's stomach with a .22 automatic. The gun had been selected for its compactness and relative quiet without a silencer, for short range rather than distance or power. Roman emerged from the confessional as the gun fired.

The .22 made less noise than a door shutting, but Isadore went down in the aisle. Roman pushed him behind a pew.

Isadore fought back. "Damn it, I'm not hit."

Light and sound had freed Reggel. He was in the south aisle, ignoring the men on the windows and galleries as he aimed straight up at Odrich. Reggel's feet were spread wide and he held the gun in both hands.

"Tell them to stop firing, colonel, or I'll kill you."

Odrich bobbed on the rope, grasping the crown. Two .22's trained on Reggel from the windows. Odrich estimated at least one would hit, but unless it took an eye or the heart the shock would be insufficient and Reggel would get his shot off.

"Captain, think. If you shoot me, what will happen to the crown?" he shouted down.

"It's been broken before. Tell them to drop the guns."

While Odrich considered, the fat officer he thought dead got to his feet. Isadore aimed his revolver at Odrich.

"No, Reggel. A trade. The Holy Crown for the cardinal. Don't move," Odrich warned as Isadore took a step forward. "Then we'll all be shooting instead of talking. After all, we have four guns to your two and the cardinal is an old man."

Reggel planted his feet more firmly and held his breath.

Odrich knew at the last moment what Reggel's decision was. He twisted his head as far to the ceiling as he could.

The sound of Reggel's gun was an explosion compared to the .22. The rope parted. Odrich held on and swung upside down into the stained-glass window. He bounced off it, spinning on the rope and still holding the crown.

There was no broken glass because the impact of Odrich's fall had been borne by the man hanging on the south window. He was still on the window, but he was no longer hanging. His broken belt sagged out of reach along the side of the window. Even Reggel lowered his gun.

The man was spread like the points of a compass against the trefoil decorations of the upper window. All that kept him from falling was the tension of his hands and heels pressed into the carved stone. From the floor, they could see his body bowing out over the sanctuary and, with the lights on, the whites of his eyes as he looked at his friend on the far window.

The man on the gallery below him tried to swing the chandelier chain closer, but Odrich was in the way.

"Jozsef," Odrich yelled up from the rope. "The belt."

The head turned slowly, refusing to become dizzy. One foot slipped and his ankle dug into the stone. He stretched his left hand. The belt was four feet away between the window and a pilaster of ribs branching out onto the ceiling.

"Jump," Odrich ordered him.

As his other foot slipped off, he jumped.

The figure turned skillfully in the air. It landed a foot too low against the ribs curving into the center of the church and clung for a second. There was a pleading look at Odrich before the desperate grip was lost and an arm outstretched for help as he dropped, but Odrich held onto the rope with one hand and the crown with the other.

The man called Jozsef landed behind the choir stall. The other climber watched, fascinated, as one of the dead man's shoes rolled all the way over the sanctuary stones to the communion rail. He tore his eyes away to look at Odrich in disbelief.

The chain was swung to the climber's hands. Winches holding the chains were thrown open and chandeliers and men began descending to the floor.

Roman and Isadore ran down one aisle to the front door, while the three who had abandoned Odrich ran down the other. Roman heard the detective shouting for him to get out of the way, but the aisles were the equivalent of a fifty-yard dash. He noticed Isadore falling farther behind. By the time the five men converged in the vestibule, Isadore was gasping like a steam engine.

First through the door was a tall blond sprinter whom Roman remembered from the convertible. Roman was next.

Two of Odrich's men came after. The second turned to aim his gun at Isadore, and the detective seized the opportunity to throw himself on the floor in what passed as a tackle. The man with the gun went down and so did his friend.

Outside, Roman and the sprinter rolled down the stairs to the sidewalk. The sprinter was up first and reached for his gun. He straightened up quickly when he saw his gun in Roman's hand.

Odrich had ridden the chain only partway down, jumping with the crown into the gallery. Reggel likewise disregarded the men landing in the sanctuary and ran to the gallery steps.

The gallery was empty when Reggel reached it. The door at the end was open. Reggel stopped where he was and fired a 7.65 slug that pierced both sides of the near air blower. Then he aimed at the far one.

Odrich darted from the second blower, shooting. He was through the open door before Reggel could pick himself up from the floor.

Where are all the detectives that are supposed to be here? the Hungarian wondered.

Behind the door was an area Reggel had been in only once before, an unlit wooden walkway leading from south gallery to north gallery in the space between the Lady Chapel's domed ceiling and its steep-pitched copper roof. There, like a worm in the skull, Odrich would wait for him to step into the light of the doorway.

Reggel pressed himself against the wall beside the door. In the sanctuary below, Killane knelt over a shoe and a sock that protruded from the choir stall.

"He's dead, cardinal. Take my word for it."

Reggel aimed at the altar. With his first shot the lights in the ambulatory dimmed. At his second the light panel shorted and the cathedral went black.

Reggel plunged through the door. The first thing he stepped on was a paint can placed in the middle of the walkway. He went down on his face but kept moving on his hands and knees until he regained his feet. Odrich's .22 popped twice. Reggel's cheek was bleeding, but whether from a bullet or his fall he didn't know.

The walkway made a 90-degree left turn at the end of the chapel. Reggel rebounded off the rail. Odrich was firing again, and Reggel felt a bullet pass through the back of his leg.

Reggel caromed off another rail, then dropped to one knee and made a quarter turn left. The noise of his automatic overwhelmed Odrich's .22 and resounded around the roof like a bell clapper. Parts of the door behind Odrich scattered into the north gallery, and at Reggel's last shot the door itself flew open.

While Reggel still squatted, he as much felt as heard Odrich climb back on the walkway and run untouched out on the gallery. Odrich's lead was no more than twenty feet, but he had vanished by the time Reggel reached the end of the gallery.

Reggel ran back the way he'd come. Beside a shattered door was a short flight of stairs. He took them in a bound and threw his arms up. A tin-and-tar-paper cover shot into the air, and Reggel heaved himself up onto the roof.

A battery of finials surrounded him on three sides. On the other was Fifty-first Street.

Reggel was about to go back in the church when he saw a flash of gold running along the upper roof. It was as if Odrich had leaped fifty feet in one jump.

Reggel found the rope he was looking for hanging beside an apsidal window. He also saw why Odrich had gone up instead of down. The street were filling with cars and police. He yanked himself up the rope greedily, his feet running over the window.

Odrich had ripped the lining from the Holy Crown and thrust his arm through it so he could use both hands climbing the slate tiles of the roof. The heavy crown still slowed him, and Reggel was already scaling the roof face when

Odrich reached the top. Unaware, Odrich moved along the five-and-a-half-foot-tall open crest of gilded brass that ran the length of the ridge.

The roof was laid out in a cross. As Odrich reached the bar he saw police cars on Fifth Avenue. For the first time he was aware of growing tired.

Reggel kept track of Odrich by the crown swinging in his hand. The crown stopped short as Odrich seemed to halt and consider his next move. Reggel inched closer, keeping the man-high crest between them.

The crown came back toward him, and Reggel crouched within an arc of the crest. There were shouts in the street, as meaningless as the lights of the skyscrapers.

Odrich stopped ten feet away to rest, setting the Holy Crown on a point of the crest.

Reggel had only started to ease forward when Odrich wheeled and shot. Although the bullet went through Reggel's chest, it was his legs that collapsed. A hand clutched to the bottom of the crest kept him from falling entirely, but his heart pounded as if it were tearing loose of its arteries. His face grew hot against the cold slate and a roaring filled his ears. He noticed as a secondary effect the blood rising to his mouth.

"It always works," Odrich said as if his point had been proven. "Show you the Holy Crown and you lose all sense. You are reliable in that way alone."

Leaning over, he placed the barrel of his gun against Reggel's temple. Before he fired, the bells of the north tower began ringing in the dark. Odrich was amused.

"The cardinal, do you think? A call for help?"

He was not so amused to find that Reggel's free hand had moved around his ankle. Odrich tried to push the hand off with his other foot, but his sneakers made it impossible to get the necessary force.

"Don't be foolish. Let go and I won't shoot."

Reggel let go of the crest and grabbed Odrich's ankle with both hands. The Hungarian was not trying to climb up. He was pulling down.

"You'll only get us both killed that way, Reggel."

Reggel got his feet planted into the roof's steep pitch

and stood, hauling on Odrich with all his strength as he swayed. His shirt and pants were red.

"You're crazy."

Odrich fired until the hammer of his gun flailed an empty chamber. He dropped the gun and twisted back to hold onto the crest with both hands but couldn't reach. The hand he had on the crest began to spread.

Reggel had hold of both Odrich's feet and seemed to be walking down the roof.

"Magyar!"

The cry came from the street only once. There was nobody near the crest or on the roof to hear a second one.

A general rush to the falling bodies carried Isadore and Lynch to the buttresses along Fiftieth Street. Men bearing stretchers and cameras followed them. One of the patrol cars used its spotlight to pick out the Holy Crown on the crest.

Roman passed them all going in the opposite direction.

CHAPTER 22

THE HORSE WAS tall and milky white. The boy held onto Roman's waist as they rode around Pulika's camp.

"You don't see many of those in the city," Isadore observed. He and Dany watched from the park next to the Gypsy's lot.

"That's why we're going, if you let us," Dany said.

"Do you know how many different investigations have started about the crown? And each one wants its hands on Roman."

They heard Pulika hoot with excitement as Roman slapped the horse into a gallop. A dog ran behind with enthusiastic barks.

"Why are you so set on going?" Isadore asked.

"It's the Gypsy in me."

He smiled painfully at Dany. "You're starting to sound like Roman. You've been around him too long."

"If I can help it."

Roman knew his hour was up. The horse galloped out of the lot and into the park, climbing the hill to where Dany and Isadore waited for him.

"Here I am, back in protective custody," he said as he slipped off the horse.

167

The boy's blue eyes amazed Dany.

"*Sarishan.*"

"*Sarishan,*" he answered her greeting.

Roman patted the horse's nose and pointed him back toward the camp.

"Take it easy," he told the boy. "He's a good horse. Just let him take you home."

The boy dug his bare feet into the horse's side. They went down the hill at a walk, but from the boy's expression they might have been racing the wind.

"I didn't know you spoke Romany," Isadore told Dany.

"I'm learning."

Isadore's Ford was parked out of sight of Pulika's camp. They walked to the car in silence. Before opening the door, the detective fumbled in his pockets until he found a stick of gum.

"The cardinal is being questioned this morning," he said. "They'll start on you as soon as we return. What happens if I lose you before then?"

Dany smartly opened her purse and took out two passports.

"What about your suitcase?" Roman asked. "We can't go back for that."

"Since when does a *chi* need suitcases?"

"Well, she's right," Isadore admitted. "She's learning."

They made their farewells on the Staten Island side of the Narrows. Roman and Dany waved down a cab to take them across the bridge to the airport.

"Is this how Gypsies really live? I think I'll like it."

Roman kissed her as their cab took them over New York Bay.

"Tell me how you like this?" he asked her.

> "Let your red blood and my red blood
> Run together in one stream,
> Let it drive a mill,
> And that mill should have three stones;
> Its first stone should throw white pearls,
> Its second stone should throw small change,
> It's third stone should produce love."

"Very much," Dany said. "Is that Gypsy?"

"No, oddly enough. That's actually Hungarian."

They had a final glimpse of Manhattan before the bridge descended to Long Island.

"Reggel taught it to you?"

"Yes," Roman lied, because he knew no one else would give Reggel an epitaph.

ABOUT THE AUTHOR

MARTIN CRUZ SMITH has written novels about American Indians and espionage as well as the Roman Grey gypsy mysteries, prior to becoming a best-selling author with his widely acclaimed *Gorky Park*. He is currently at work on a novel about New Mexico.